Praise for

I M A N I   A L L   M I N E :

"Beautifully realized...captivating."
— *New York Times Book Review*

"She finds grace notes in her characters' dogged endurance,
always letting light shine through lamentable lives."
— *Boston Globe*

"An unsparing, remarkably unsentimental tale
of a typically unsung heroine."
— *Kirkus Reviews*

"Porter's candid narrative will have you hooked
from the opening sentence."
— *Seventeen*

"Full of humor, joy, sadness,
hopeful innocence, and gritty realism."
— *Library Journal*

"Elegant, moving."
— *Pittsburgh Post-Gazette*

Books by Connie Porter

◆

ALL-BRIGHT COURT

IMANI ALL MINE

IMANI
ALL MINE

Connie Porter

A Mariner Book

HOUGHTON MIFFLIN COMPANY

Boston   New York

I wish to thank my family and friends, whose support and love have sustained me through the writing of this book. I would also like to thank my editor, Janet Silver, whose vision and insight guided me to the place where I could hear Tasha's voice clearly.

First Mariner Books edition 2000

Copyright © 1999 by Connie Porter

Visit our Web site: www.hmco.com/trade.

Library of Congress Cataloging-in-Publication Data
Porter, Connie Rose, date.
Imani all mine / Connie Porter.
p. cm.
ISBN 0-395-83808-8   ISBN 0-618-05678-5 (pbk.)
1. Afro-Americans — New York (State) —
Buffalo — Fiction. I. Title.
PS3566.O6424I63   1999
813'.54 — dc21   98-37722   CIP

Book Design by Anne Chalmers
Typeface: Adobe Garamond

Printed in the United States of America

QUM 20 19 18 17 16 15 14 13 12

For Nicole, Tia, LaMont, Chauvonne, and Ty

Chance made you sisters and brothers,
but love made you friends forever

NOW FAITH IS THE SUBSTANCE OF
THINGS HOPED FOR, THE EVIDENCE
OF THINGS NOT SEEN.

—Hebrews 11:1

ONE

Say, Say, Say

Mama say I'm grown now because I got Imani. She say Imani all mine. I know she all mine, and I like it just like that, not having to share my baby with no one. Imani even look like me. I know she do, got my nose on her face, and my lips, my hands. Her fingers shaped just like mine, wide and flat. I don't care what nobody say, who they say they might see in her. It's only me in her.

When I be getting up with her at night, it be my own face looking back at me. I want to be mad at her because it be two o'clock in the morning. Imani so little she don't know when it's a weekend, and I ain't got to get up and go nowhere. She don't know when it's a weekday, and I be having to get up and go to school. It's high school now. Lincoln. I got to get there a whole hour earlier than I had to get to middle school. But I don't be mad at Imani when I look her in the face and see me. I be smiling at her. Real quick I go to her, because Mama done told me she don't want to hear Imani crying. She say she going to get me if she cry too much.

Even though I done had her just five months, I got things

down right. It's what you call a routine. Before Imani can let out one good scream, my feet be on the floor. Sometimes it seem I still be sleep, but I go pick her up from her crib. She still light, like a doll or a puppy. It seem like she was heavier when she was inside my stomach.

I press her face against my shoulder and take her downstairs to fix her bottle. Imani a good baby. A real good baby. She know she got to be quiet, so when I hold her head against my titties, she hush right up. She don't want to see me get in no trouble. While the bottle heat up, I walk with her around the kitchen. She like that. It's like she even know the routine. We walk around in the dark kitchen with that tiny blue flame dancing under the pot on the stove.

I take her in the living room and punch on the TV. There don't be nothing on. Our cable done been cut off. Even our illegal cable that June Bug had climbed up the pole and hooked up for us. One day last year I was coming home from school and seen this white man from the cable company up on a pole cutting wires left and right. Some of our neighbors was peeping out they curtains. But they ain't come out. Not even June Bug. I seen him like a shadow pressed inside his screen door, watching that cable man cut down the pair of sneakers that was hanging on the wires in front of his house. June Bug wait for the cable man to leave and he went and got them sneakers and tied them back together. I heard this boy on the bus say once drug dealers be hanging up sneakers in front of they houses. That sound stupid to me. Like they advertising. Everybody know June Bug sell drugs. He don't need no sneakers announcing it.

Me and Mama was sitting out on the front porch, watching him and not watching him. We was drinking us some good sweet and cold Kool-Aid and eating salt-and-vinegar potato chips. June Bug kept tossing them sneakers. Seem like he had two wounded gray and nasty-looking birds folded up in his hands. Trying to get them back up into the sky. He threw them up about ten times and they come crashing back to the ground. This little cockeye boy that live down at the corner with his grandma come running up the street and say he could toss them sneakers up there. I thought he going to clunk hisself in the head. But he got them sneakers up on a telephone wire in just two throws with his cockeye self.

June Bug say, You all right little man. In a few years I'm going to have you working for me. He give that boy some money, and that boy went racing back down the street.

Mama say it was a shame, because June Bug the one got that boy mama all strung out in the first place on that stuff. That's how come he living with his grandma in the second place.

I ain't say nothing about them. I ask Mama about the cable.

She say, What you want me to do? I'm sick of this shit. That's the second time they done come and cut the cable.

I say, You can pay the bill.

Mama say, If I had money to pay the goddamn bill in the first place, we wouldn't have to bootleg.

When I told Mama maybe we could get June Bug to go back up the pole, she roll her eyes at me and suck her teeth. Huh, she say. I ain't paying no more damn twenty dollars for nobody to go up no pole to turn around and ain't got no service. We watching whatever come on for free.

So when I be watching our old boring stone-age TV at night with Imani, ain't even no point in turning on the sound. The light help keep me awake while Imani nurse. She be greedy at first, like she ain't had a bottle in years. Maybe it seem like years to her. Sometimes I don't know all what's inside her head, what she understand. I go to this class, though. It teach you more about a baby.

My middle school counselor signed me up for it last spring after Imani was born and got her in the daycare. I like that. Having her close by all day. Knowing she just down on the first floor with the other babies. Mama say when she went to school, there wasn't no classes like them. There wasn't no nurseries in high schools. Maybe there should have been. Mama say you took care of your baby the best way you knew how. Mama say me and the other girls is spoiled. That is all. Plain and simple. We got things too easy.

Most of the girls who got babies in the nursery take the class. They even got girls in there that is going to have babies. My friend Eboni going to have a baby. She barely seven months, but she look like she about ready to deliver.

Me and Eboni sit together. Our seats right in the front of the room, and we don't like the teacher, Mrs. Poole. Her breath stink, flat out. That shouldn't make you not like a person, but it sure make them hard to listen to, especially when they be all up in your face. Mrs. Poole like that; she be all up in your face telling you how to wipe shit off a baby butt, and you can really imagine doing it because her breath smell like some shit you can't just wipe away with a moist towelette.

Mrs. Poole the one told me about "establishing a routine" with Imani. She say babies like routines. They act better if they know what to expect. I believe that's true about Imani. She so smart, she learned her routine quick. But I don't know if all Mrs. Poole say true. Maybe it's because I be half-listening, because I'm trying to dodge her breath. Like she say, a baby bond with you, a baby bond with its mother. Mrs. Poole say a baby ain't born loving its mother. I swear that's what she say last week. I ask Eboni after school was that what she say, and Eboni say it was. Mrs. Poole say you got to teach a baby to love you. Now, I think that ain't even true. Imani was born loving me.

The crazy thing was, I wasn't loving Imani all along. Loving her every minute because I was scared. Mama thought I was hiding Imani from her. It's just like Mama to think that. She only knew part of the truth. I was hiding her from myself. I didn't even know she was there inside my stomach until I missed my fourth period. Eboni say she knew before I even told her. We was in the same gym class, and Eboni say she could see my stomach growing.

When I told her one day after gym was over, Eboni say she thought it might not be too late to get rid of it. Get rid of it? I ain't like the way that sound, like the baby was just going to be throwed out. I ain't want that and told Eboni so. She ask, What you want then? To give it away? I shook my head. Eboni put her arms around me, and you'd think that'd be enough to stop me from getting upset. But I went crazy crying and couldn't stop. The gym teacher come in and say I could go to the nurse, but I ain't want to go. I was thinking the nurse would look right at me and see I had a baby in me. Then she'd tell Mama. Then I'd get beat.

My gym teacher let me and Eboni go in her office and stay there up until the next bell. She wrote a note saying I was hit in the head with a ball and was laying down for a period. I don't know what she wrote for Eboni. I wasn't crying no more when the bell rang. Wasn't no more tears. Eboni promised she wouldn't tell nobody, but she say I had to tell Mama. But I say I couldn't and she knew I couldn't. Mama'd say I been doing nasty things with boys. I'm not nasty.

Sometimes I think Imani had a routine before she even come out of me. Every night she'd wake me up at just about this same time. She'd be moving around. I would hold my breath, keeping real still until she stopped. I was stupid enough to think she could punch a hole in my stomach and come right on out me. Maybe she just wanted to remind me she was in there, because I was doing my best to forget.

Carrying her mostly through winter and into a Buffalo spring that's just like winter, I wore these big sweats. It wasn't hard to keep her a secret. My stomach never really poked out much, anyway. I just kept getting fatter from eating so much. I don't really like Mama's cooking, but I don't say that to her, because she'll say I'm ungrateful for all she do for me, and slap me.

Mostly when I was carrying Imani, I'd go to Eboni's after school. Her mama, Miss Lovey, a good cook. I think Eboni told her about the baby. I ain't saying Eboni is the kind of loud-mouth girl who tell all your business. She ain't like one of them girls on the bus. You give them a bone on the way to school, and on the bus ride back, they done already showed it to every bitch they know and they all trying to get a lick off it.

Miss Lovey ain't say nothing to me. She just pile my plate up real high with food, with liver and onions, lasagna loaded up with them hot Italian sausage, and her greens. They the best. She rinse her greens real good. Don't be nam grain of sand in them, and she cook them with two kinds of meat, ham hocks and bacon, and she season them just right, with hot sauce and vinegar. Thinking about them even now make my stomach flip.

Miss Lovey ain't never ask me nothing about me having a baby. She would push a extra biscuit on my plate, pour me a big glass of buttermilk, slip a piece of fat meat on my plate she know I like. Sometimes she'd look at me with that look adults have, the one where they know you got a secret and they want you to tell them so they can slide into a seat next to you and pat your hand or rub your back while you spill your guts out to them.

I looked right back at Miss Lovey when she looked at me like that. I give her that I-know-you-know-I-got-a-secret look, but I ain't going to say it. Why I got to say it when she already know what it was?

Mama ain't even know about Imani until one morning when I ain't get up for school on time. I was all tired because Imani had kept me up kicking and moving around all night. I guess she was tired of being in me. And these cramps was pinching in my back. They was soft at first like my period was coming, but then they got harder. I finally took me three aspirins real late. I only got a hour of sleep by the time the alarm went off. It's right by my bed, so I shut it off, but I didn't get up. I should've like I do now with the routine. I should've let my feet hit the floor and start walking without me. It seem like I just closed my eyes when I heard Mama up. I looked at the clock. It was five minutes before the bus come. I thought I could make it if I wore the sweats I slept in and just wiped a rag over my face and run out the door. But my sweats was too funky so I started to change them when Mama opened my room door.

I was standing there in my drawers. I didn't even have my

bra on yet. I ain't say nothing. I ain't have to. My titties say it. They was as big as watermelons. My stomach say it. It was all stretched wide, spread out around my body. I know I looked ugly, even though I ain't looked at myself in a mirror in a long time. Not even on my birthday, the month before.

I was fifteen on my birthday. I wasn't all that excited about turning fifteen. Fourteen neither. Last time I was excited about my birthday was when I turned thirteen and I was finally a teenager. They always be having them articles in *Seventeen* about how great it is to be old enough to wear makeup, how to dress for the prom, what twenty pieces of clothes you got to have to go back to school in the fall, how to tell if a boy like you. I ain't think I was going to look like them girls in there, all skinny and all, but I did think I might feel like them. Happy. And I was. We had a ice cream cake and subs delivered. Mama got me a card. The card say something about being a teenager now. It was a joke card with a white girl on the front talking on the phone, and a corny rhyme inside.

I wasn't expecting nothing for my birthday this year. Mama just give me money last year, twenty dollars in my hand. So I wasn't looking forward to nothing great this year. What's so special about being fifteen? But what I ain't count on was Mama hitting the number. She did the Pick Four on my birth date. Month and year.

Mama give me a real nice birthday. I would've liked it if she'd just turned the cable back on. But Mama went all out for me. She got me ice cream and a cake, a real bakery cake with candles on it. She let Eboni come over. We ordered a bucket of Buffalo wings and pizza with anything I wanted on it. I got double cheese, ham, pepperoni, and hot sausage. Miss Odetta come over, too. She June Bug mama.

Eboni give me these gold earrings with my name on them. They not real gold. They that fake gold them Arabians be selling down in the Main Place Mall. The earrings nice, though. They ain't turn my ears green or make break out or nothing. Miss Odetta give me a card with twenty dollars in it. Mama give me a new pair of sneakers. Nikes. She paid some real money for them, or maybe she got them hot. I ain't ask. I needed some new kicks. My feet been growing, so I'm glad to have them. Mama give me a card, too.

It had a black mama and girl on the front. The girl was little, sitting in her mama lap. On the front of the card was *To my darling, beautiful daughter on her birthday*. On the inside it didn't rhyme. It say, *May all the joy in the world be with you on this very special day*. It was signed *Mama*. I closed it real quick and stuffed it in my sneakers.

Before I went to bed that night, I laced up my sneakers so I could show them off at school the next day. Then I did something I shouldn't have. I opened the card from Mama and read it again. I started crazy crying again, like I did that day at school.

That card was lying on me. I wasn't none of those things it say I was. I didn't have to look at myself to know that, to know how ugly and broke-down I looked. All these stretch marks running crazy over me. For months they had been on my titties, on my stomach. It looked like I was going to crack open and something was going to come from inside me, not just the baby, but something else, like in a horror movie where there be monsters in people and they don't even know it.

I hated Mama for buying that stupid card. At the same

time I wanted to go to her that night and tell her everything. I was just so sick of trying to hide my baby. I figured maybe her heart might be soft, with it still being my birthday. But when I got up, I felt Imani kick me. It seemed like she was saying for me to shut up. It's not the right time. I couldn't shut up, though. So I lay down and pushed my face deep in the pillow.

When I be crying crazy like that, all these strange noises be coming out my mouth. They be coming from deep inside me from a place I don't even know, from a place I don't even want to know. I stayed right in my bed until I quieted down all by myself, until when I opened my mouth ain't nothing come out but my breath.

Who know, maybe I should've told Mama that night. I should've say something while my heart was soft, and maybe hers was soft, too. It would have been better that way, with me just saying it, flat out, instead of her seeing me like that the morning I was late for school.

Mama ain't say nothing. She just flew right at me and slapped me in the face. I was too clumsy and slow to get out the way of her hand. Next, she punched me right in the titties. I put my hands up so she couldn't hit me no more, and I backed up and fell on the bed. Mama started asking me questions she ain't even give me time to answer, and every time she ask one, she slapped me again.

What the hell wrong with you? What was you thinking about, doing this? Why you throw your life away? What you think your aunt going to think of you? What am I going to tell her? Why you ain't tell me? Why you ain't tell me? Why you ain't tell me?

It was like Mama to think what I done was all about her, like I done something to her. I couldn't hardly tell myself, but

I couldn't say that to Mama. That wouldn't make no sense to her, so I rolled over and put my back to her. I wasn't thinking about her so much as I was thinking about my baby. I had to protect my baby.

That's why I think Mrs. Poole wrong with her stink breath. Because Imani loved me right *then*. I could feel it. I ain't have to wait for her to be born for her to love me. I ain't have to wait for her to be born to love her. She my baby.

Mama kept on asking and slapping. Who the father? What nigger you had the baby with? What's his name?

I ain't say nothing. I just curled myself up around my baby. I couldn't say his name to Mama. I couldn't even say it to myself.

Finally she ask me, without a slap, You happy now? Then she let me alone. She wasn't getting nothing out of me. She left the room and I got up and dressed real quick. I'd missed my school bus, but I could still take the city bus and not miss all of first period. I was relieved it was over, that Mama knew. She ain't really hurt me. I just wanted to get to school.

When I left the house, Mama was in her room. She ain't even come out, which was just fine with me. She was probably still sitting in there when the school nurse called her to tell her my water broke.

I ain't even know what it was. I was in my second-period math class with Mr. Crowley. He this white man who's all sucked-up looking and he got these brown teeth all piled on top of each other. He don't never leave the overhead projector where he be scribbling out problems and they solutions.

I felt like I had to go to the bathroom real bad and I could hardly hold it. I was waving my hand real wild, but Mr. Crowley ain't even look at me. He was explaining how to turn fractions into decimals and decimals into fractions. He finally called on me after I called out his name, and ask me to solve the problem. I told him I had to go to the lavatory, and you know what he had the nerve to tell me? I couldn't go. He had already give out two lavatory passes. I swear, that's the craziest thing I ever heard. He only give two bathroom passes a period because he think we be trying to go to the bathroom just to miss class. Maybe that's all right for boys, but don't he know what girls be having to do in the lavatory sometimes? Don't he think we might need more than two passes during class? I wasn't stutting Mr. Crowley and his rules just then. I got up and headed for the door. Soon as I started walking, I was dripping. I could feel it. By the time I made it out the door, I was starting to gush, and the lavatory was way at the end of the hall. Mr. Crowley was right behind me. He seen it, too. My sweat pants was stained dark. I was so embarrassed. Mr. Crowley grabbed me by the shoulders and ask me if I was all right. I told him I want to go to the lavatory, but he say he was taking me to see the nurse. I think he knew the baby was coming. I ain't want to go, but I knew I should, so he walked with me leaning on him and told me everything would be fine, and I was thinking he was wishing he had just give me a lavatory pass when I ask for one.

The nurse is this black lady. I had never even been in her office before, just past it. She called a ambulance. Then she phoned Mama and tell her to meet us at ECMC.

That's the county hospital. Some people don't like it because it's the welfare hospital, but it's all right with me. I was born there.

I wasn't really even scared until I heard the ambulance come up with that siren going. I ain't want to get in it, but the nurse say it was the best and safest way for me. She say she was going to be with me all the way. She was real calm. Her breath was even calm. It smelled like peppermint. She say she had three children and I would be fine. All the way to the hospital she sat next to me, patting my hand while the ambulance attendant ask me a bunch a questions about my prenatal care, how advanced my pregnancy was, when was my last period. I knew I ain't give the right answers by the way he was frowning.

The cramps I had the night before was back. They was harder and longer. The nurse told me to breathe, like I wasn't breathing or something. She ask how bad the pain was. I told her it wasn't that bad, and it wasn't.

Mama was there when I got to the hospital, looking real worried. I ain't know if she was worried because she hit me that morning and she thought these people would find out about it, or if she was really worried about me. When they wheeled me past her, I looked in her face. It looked like she was really worried about me. It looked like she been crying.

They took me in this cold room and I was all naked. There was nothing but this sheet over me. Some nurse come in and give me a shot. This doctor come and stood over me. He was from some other country. I don't know where, but he had a funny accent. He say they was going to take the baby out of me, just to be safe. I tell him I could take the pain, but he say they want to be safe. You're just a child, he say to me.

That's all I remember until after Imani was born. I don't know what they give me, but the next thing I know, it was dark outside and I was in this room with some other women with babies. Mama was sitting in a chair next to my bed, her arms folded on her chest, and she was staring at a television hung up on the wall. *Jeopardy!* was on. Mama ain't say nothing. She walked around the bed and took Imani out the little plastic crib they had her in. Mama handed her right to me.

I ain't know what to do. I just stared at her, feeling how light she was, looking to see who was in her face. It was only me I seen there, and when she poked one of her hands out the blanket, I seen them flat fingers like mine. I smiled.

Imani wasn't even her name then. Not official. It say *Dawson, Girl* on her ankle band. Eboni had give me that name. She got this baby book from a black card shop and it had that name in it. She was picking out names after she found out she was having a baby. She told me what Imani mean in some African language. Faith. I liked that.

It seem like Mama want to say something to me, but she ain't know what say. She say I could get some ice chips, but I ain't want them. She say she needed to go home. She was tired. I told her that was all right, she could go. I had Imani.

Every time I go to Mrs. Poole class, I be learning more of what to do with Imani. I know that after the bottle, I got to burp her. Imani like that, I think. She like me patting her back. Her head be wobbling all around. I hold her head like Mrs. Poole say, but I think my baby just plain nosey. She be looking all around when I be burping her, even at two in the morning, like there's something to see.

Just last week when we was up, Imani was looking around when she heard these gunshots. Then she got real still. It was like she was holding her breath. I couldn't feel no breath coming from her. All I could feel was her heart beating fast fast. Mrs. Poole done taught us how to do CPR, but all I could think to do was give her a good shake. I knew I ain't need to when she turned and looked at me like she had a question. I felt a breath come out of her then. Hot and wet in my face. I heard the shots, too. We was on the couch, but I stopped right then patting her back and got down on the floor. I don't even want to sound dramatic, like I dove down on the floor or something. They be shooting around here sometimes at night. But the shots sound like they did that night. Like they a few blocks over. They was still loud, so I slid off onto the floor. I ain't want to scare Imani.

Mrs. Poole would probably say I'm crazy. Ain't no way a baby know what gunshots is. I ain't saying Imani knew, but that kind of scared me. After she let out a good burp, I laid Imani out on the floor and finished up the routine. I changed her diaper, wiped her off with one of them moist towelettes, and greased and powdered her butt. She got real pretty skin. She ain't had no diaper rash or nothing yet, and I'm going see to it she don't.

Imani act like she still ain't want to go to sleep that night. She wasn't fussing or nothing, but I guess she wasn't ready to go on off to sleep. So I laid down on the floor and put her up on my chest.

Mrs. Poole say that can calm a baby down. The baby hear your heart beating like when they was inside you. So I put her on my heart and sung her this song me and Eboni used to sing when we was girls. It's a hand-clapping song, but Imani can't do the clapping part yet, so I ain't do the clapping part. I don't know why I sung it, but it just come to my mind, and I sung it real soft. I sung it like a whisper.

Say, Say, Say—
I am a pretty little
Black girl

As pretty as pretty can
Be-e
And all the boys around my block are crazy over
Me-e
My boyfriend's name is
Sam-bo
He comes from A-la-
Bam-a
With a pickle on his nose and a cherry on his toes
That's why my story goes.

TWO

All in Together, Girls

I'M A NASTY GIRL now. That's what Mama would say if she knew me and Peanut been doing it. I figure she helped make me a nasty girl, if that's what I really am. She the one put me on birth control pills after she found out Eboni was pregnant.

I ain't want to be on no pills. I ain't need them none, but what you going to tell Mama? When she say she already had done made a appointment for me at ECMC and my fast black ass was going to get on them goddamn pills before I got me another baby, wasn't nothing I could say. She say Eboni probably give me the idea to get pregnant from in the first place, because she ain't nothing but a stinking little ho. My back was to Mama when she was saying them things, because I was bathing Imani in the kitchen sink.

Mrs. Poole say that's the best place to bathe a baby so you can keep a good hold of it. Mrs. Poole say a baby can drown in less than a inch of water. It scared me when she say that. My mind left right from that classroom, and I could see Imani clear as day drowned in her little plastic yellow tub I been bathing her in. Mrs. Poole was standing over me, looking at my notebook. She could see I underlined that part about the drowning, that I was paying attention.

I was holding on to Imani real tight when Mama was talking at me that day. She was holding me real tight right back. Like she know there was some danger in the water, but she know I ain't never going to let nothing happen to her. I was glad I had my back to Mama, because no matter how hard I tried to fix my face right, it was telling the truth on me, and if I turned around I'd get a good smack for being so goddamn disrespectful. Mrs. Poole say you want respect from your child, give respect to your child.

That idea ain't go over real hot with the girls in our class. A lot of girls sucked they teeth and rolled they eyes at Mrs. Poole. This girl Bett-Bett, who always be sitting in the far back seat, say that was some bullshit. Now Mrs. Poole ain't like the rest of the teachers. She don't be writing you up for cussing or nothing, but she remind you cussing is for ignorant people with little minds. If you say sorry like you mean it, Mrs. Poole let it slide and let you say what you have to say like a lady would. Bett-Bett say she sorry and then she say to Mrs. Poole that things is the other way around. Children got to respect they elders. Bett-Bett say if her two kids want respect from her, they better show respect to her first.

Mrs. Poole ain't do nothing but ask a question. Don't I respect you? Bett-Bett ain't say nothing. We was all looking at Bett-Bett too, and some girls was saying yes. Mrs. Poole respect us. Mrs. Poole wave her hands for us to hush. She say she was asking Bett-Bett. You could tell Bett-Bett ain't want to admit it, because there was some kind of lecture coming, but she sunk down in her seat and say yes. Mrs. Poole walk right back to Bett-Bett and put both her hands on her shoulders. *I* respected *you* from the day you walked into my class, Mrs. Poole say. I set the example. Let me tell you, ladies, Mrs. Poole say. You must respect your children. It's they right to be respected. They birthright. You have to set the example and teach them what respect is by being respectful yourself.

I'm sure Bett-Bett was melting under Mrs. Poole stank breath, but she ain't show it. It seem like she was really listening to her. I think we all was, because sometime Mrs. Poole be making good sense, the kind of sense you know be right.

And what she say about respect was burning me up the day Mama told me about going on them pills. I kept washing Imani longer than I needed to, waiting for my face to get right. I mean, Eboni ain't no ho, no matter what Mama say. Mama don't even know her, not really. And I ain't even get no idea of having a baby from Eboni. Like Imani some idea. A baby ain't no idea somebody put in your head. Maybe Eboni be putting ideas in my head about a new style to braid my hair in or what new sneakers everybody wearing. But can't nobody put a baby in your head.

Imani was looking up at me like she knew I was thinking something. She start kicking the water out the sink. She ain't never been in the water so long. It was getting cold, so I rinsed her off and took her on upstairs. I ain't have to face Mama. She was watching TV.

I oiled up Imani real good until she was shining and put lots of powder on her butt. I swear that look funny. The oil with the powder over it. It look like when you flour and grease a cake pan. After I diapered and dressed her, we lay down on my bed and listened to the radio. I put on WBLK.

My baby like that. She like rap. She shake her head to it. On time.

I ain't even come out the room until I had to give Imani her late feeding. We stayed the rest of the night on the couch and I ain't felt like getting up and going to no doctor the next morning.

While Imani was still sleeping, I took me a long shower. I scrubbed my private parts real good, because the doctor would probably be looking at them and poking them, and I ain't want to be stank. I can't stand no doctor looking in them places no way. It make me all embarrassed.

I dropped Imani off at her daycare before me and Mama went to the doctor's. I ain't had nothing to eat, but the whole while me and Mama was sitting in the waiting room, I felt this clenching like in my guts. I thought I was going to have to poop. When we was called in to see the doctor and I had to put on that paper gown, I felt even worse. This one nurse had me pee in a little jar. She took some blood and then weighed me. I had gained almost ten pounds since my six-week checkup, but she say my pressure was fine. The nurse left me and Mama to wait on the doctor. I was sitting on the examining table. My stomach was bubbling like a pot. Mama heard it. She ask what's wrong with me. I say I was nervous about the doctor looking at my private parts. She say I ain't care nothing about some boy fucking me, so what I care about some doctor taking a look. I was going to cry right then, but the doctor walked in.

For some reason, that made me calm. It was a black woman doctor and she pretty. Her hair was done real nice. She must have had one of them relaxers, where you can shake your hair like a white woman, and her hair was real long.

Mama smiled at her real big. The doctor ask me why I wasn't in school that morning. Because I'm here, I say. That's obvious, she say in a real flat voice, not even looking up from my file. Your weight is up, she say. It's not healthy to weigh so much. Don't you exercise? I be tired, I say, which is the truth. You a young girl, she tell me. You shouldn't be tired. You tired because you overweight. She say she run five miles every day. All the while she say these things, she didn't even look at me. She didn't even look at me when she ask, Why you have a baby so young? I swear I felt like jumping off that table and smacking her. Ain't none of her business why I have a baby. Mama say, That's what I want to know. The doctor looked at her and they started talking about me like I wasn't even there.

She don't listen to me, Mama say. The doctor say she see it every day, babies having babies. It's getting to be more than she can take. Mama say she try to tell me what's right, but I be getting ideas from other girls. That your daughter? Mama ask, pointing at a picture on the doctor's desk. The doctor smiled. Mama show me the picture. The girl looked around my age, and was dressed in a prom dress. She real pretty, Mama say. The doctor thanked her for saying that. That's her debutante picture.

She turn to me and say, That's where your daughter comes out, gets presented to society. Talking to me like I was some natural-born fool. I know what a debutante is, but I ask her, Where she come out from? The doctor just look at me real strange, and Mama glared at me.

Then Mama say it's so good to see a black girl who's about something, doing something with they lives instead of having babies like that's some great thing. Because it ain't.

I had my face fixed real plain while they carried on talking. Like they was talking about something like the best place to get your hair fixed or what place sell the best Buffalo wings. But I was burning up. My thighs was sticking to that paper they be having on them examining tables, and my feet tingling from hanging up in the air. I ain't give a damn about that doctor or her stupid-ass daughter. I know Mrs. Poole would say I'm no lady for expressing myself that way, even if it was all inside my head. That my mind was real little. But I ain't even care. That girl ain't mean nothing to me. I ain't know why Mama was making over her like she's something special.

She look like a regular black girl to me. Her skin dark like mine. She ain't have no good hair or nothing. She's not fat like me, but she's not pretty like them black girls in *Seventeen*. If you seen her on the street, you would probably throw her all in together with other black girls. You would think she was probably a ho. Like mama think I am. You would think she was probably stupid. You would think she was nothing.

The doctor say too many of *our* girls throwing they lives away, giving up on they futures.

Mama say that ain't going to happen to me. That's why she brung me for the pills. Tasha a smart girl. Get all A's.

Really? the doctor ask. That's the first time she act like she was interested in me, like I was more than some fat-ass dumb ugly black girl.

The doctor smiled at me, this real phony fake plastic smile, and Mama carried on. Tasha came out of her middle school class with the second highest average. She won the science certificate and the reading certificate and was on the honor roll every term. Tasha been on the honor roll every marking period but one in high school. She back on it now, Mama say. Mama was smiling this real smile.

I swear Mama so pretty when she smile. Her skin so dark and smooth. She be looking young when she smile. Mama say she was protecting my future by putting me on the pills.

I couldn't keep my face flat no more. I was smiling back. Mama ain't one to brag on me much, but when she do, I be liking it. Sometimes I hear her talking on the phone to Aunt Mavis, telling her about my report card. It's like she really proud of me, and I'm that girl on the birthday card or one of them girls in *Seventeen* who got good self-esteem and one of them skinny bodies with neat little titties.

I swear, for the first time that doctor talked to me like I had some sense. What you want to be when you grow up? she ask me. I told her a nurse, a nurse who work with children, because I love children. She ask, You ever thought about being a pediatrician? I ask, A doctor? Then I felt like a fool, like I ain't know what a pediatrician is. I threw in right quick that I been thinking about being a *pediatric* nurse, because it take such a long time to be a doctor. Then she smiled a real smile at me and say time is one thing I got plenty of. But I got to take care of myself. Take care of my body. Not having no more babies was a way to start.

She explained how them pills worked and not to miss one day. I felt like telling her I ain't really need them because I wasn't doing it, like I was going to tell Mama. It seem like the doctor might have listened. Maybe Mama, too. But I ain't say nothing, and I'm glad I ain't, because I'm doing it now.

I met Peanut at school a few weeks later. This is the thing. I wasn't stutting him when I first seen him. He was put in my homeroom because his was too crowded. Miss Williams, our homeroom teacher, had him standing up in the front of the room when we come in one morning. He short and skinny. She say his name Clyde Baker Junior. She ask him if he want to say something.

He say, Yeah, don't call me Clyde. Call me Peanut. Why they call you Peanut? Reuben ask. Why you think? Kente say. He got a head shape just like a big old peanut.

We was all laughing. I felt bad about laughing when I seen Peanut looking like he was going to cry. Miss Williams say that was enough. She made Kente apologize to Peanut. She say she was calling him Clyde, and the rest of us could call him what we want. She give him a seat next to Reuben.

I only got lunch and gym with Peanut, because I take the Regents courses and he don't. Regents classes real hard. But they ain't as crowded as regular classes like health. There thirty-three of us in health, stuffed in a room with no window. I think the room used to be a closet. The desks so close together, your knees be just about touching the kid's butt in front of you. And it be so funky. A whole group of boys come in right after they gym period, and they underarms just about choke you to death. But in Latin, there's twelve. Pre-Algebra, twenty. Honors English, seventeen. Physical Science, twenty-five.

Even though the girls and boys have gym during the same period, we don't always be doing the same things. When Peanut first come, the boys was playing this stupid game called handball in the gym. The girls was doing double dutch outside. Most of the girls.

Some boys come out and jumped with us some of the time. But this one sissy boy, Franklin, jumped with us all the time. Franklin don't even be bothering with the other boys much. They beat him up and call him faggot and call him a girl. But the girls don't be doing that. Franklin don't be bothering nobody. He jump on a team and even been down to New York City jumping in tournaments. Them other boys jealous of him, I think.

About a week into our jumping, Peanut and Reuben and Kente come busting out the side door of the gym and tried to bogart our jump-rope game. The teacher wasn't nowhere around. Kente say, A bunch of girls and a faggot can jump, can't be nothing to it. We let him and the others try so we could see them look stupid.

These girls, Yvette and Coco, was turning them ropes so fast, they humming and kicking up dirt. Then they start singing:

> All, all, all in together, girls
> How you like the weather, girls?

All us girls was lined up. We answered they call jumping in one by one when they called out our birth month until we was in the ropes. Even Franklin. The boys started laughing when he jumped in. But he ain't even seem to care. All the girls was laughing, and he was laughing, too.

We was all jumping fine until that clumsy-foot Kente jumped in and stopped the rope. He ain't even get one jump.

We let the boys have they try. One by one, Kente was first. Slow them ropes down, he say. Ya'll trying to kill me?

Look here, Yvette say. She and Coco slow the ropes down. This here baby speed. Kente cry like a baby. *Waah. Waah. Waah.* I'm scared, he say.

I know you scared, Yvette say. Kente jumped in swinging

his hands in front of him like he was in a fight. Out. We all laughed at him.

Them ropes can't hit back, Coco say.

They do, Kente say, and one cut me right on my ass. You want to kiss it and make it better? he ask Coco. I swear, he always got something smart to say. Kente patted hisself. Not in the back either. In the front.

Coco say, Get away from me, you nasty boy. She was smiling when she say that. She like Kente. Everybody know that. I don't even know why. Coco real pretty. Chocolate just like cocoa. She look like some little doll. While Kente look like something you scrape from under the bottom of your foot.

Next come Reuben. He want to start in the ropes. This ain't no kindergarten, I say. You can't be starting in no ropes. Give him baby speed, too, this other girl say. I swear, for a whole minute he was rocking back and forth like he was getting set to jump in. I could tell he ain't know what he was doing.

My grandma could get in these ropes, Coco say, and she walk on a cane.

Shit or get off the pot, Kente say. Then Reuben jumped in. He jumped once, and Kente and Peanut started screaming like he had done something great. Reuben got another chance and missed right off.

It was Peanut turn then. He stood way off from them ropes like they was going to bite him. Then he jumped clean in and out the ropes without getting touched. We tried to get him to go back in, but he wouldn't go.

Kente want to come in again, but we wouldn't let him. I took over turning for Coco, and me and Yvette put some pepper to them ropes. Coco skinny like a boy and she jump the fastest. Her little bony legs be moving double-time. She got out when she tried to do a split jump, and then Franklin went. I squatted down, and he flew right over my head and did a flip into the ropes. He jumped on all fours. He jumped holding on to one foot. He did three three-sixties in a row and was out on the fourth. Even Kente had to say, Boy, you bad. Franklin was all cool about it when he took my end of the rope. He ain't even crack a smile.

I was next. I ain't had no big tricks like him and Coco. The ropes still had the pepper in them, and I leaped on in. I got my rhythm going and threw in some foot crosses. I still look down for them even though I shouldn't. I was starting my one-foot spins when all this screaming started. I turned right around, and there was Peanut in the ropes, jumping like a jumping fool.

Peanut did a three-sixty and Franklin say, Go, Clyde, go Clyde. Then they was all saying it. All but Peanut. He was saying, Go, Tasha, go, Tasha. He grabbed my hands and had this real big smile on his face. Then I seen where his eyes was. Right on my titties.

My titties was bouncing up and down, and I was so embarrassed that I get out on purpose. I was so glad when the bell rang. I flew into the building without looking back.

The next gym class, I thought Peanut was going to forget all about me. Him and Reuben nem ain't come and join us jumping. When I got a chance, I peeped inside the gym. It was sunny bright out, so when I looked inside, the gym was kind of dark. I could make out Peanut running fast-fast with not one thought of me in his head. He ain't even look my way. But he come sit across from me at my lunch table and put a ice cream sandwich on my tray. You want it? he ask. I got me a extra. I ain't even answer that nasty boy. Coco was sitting at the table. I'll eat it, she say. I had to slap her hand off my tray. As skinny as she is, she eat more than me. I unwrapped the sandwich and began eating it. Coco ask Peanut where he learn to jump so good. He say he got a older sister, she in college now, he learned from her.

Where you live, Tasha? Peanut ask me.

I ain't telling you where I live, I say.

Peanut say, Kente tell me you live right round the block from me.

Look, I say, you tell Kente keep my name out his mouth.

I ask him where you live, Peanut say.

What you want to know for? I ask.

He say he just want to know, then looked down at his tray. He got these real long eyelashes and I was noticing how pretty they was. Black and shiny and thick. He ain't look at me right away. He was opening his ice cream sandwich.

Why you called Peanut? I ask.

He looked at me and smiled.

He say it was because he was born so little. They ain't know if he was going to live. He was only three pounds and some ounces because he was premature. He say he couldn't breathe so good. He say his whole body could fit in his daddy hand. He kept on talking, but I wasn't listening so good, because I was picturing him hardly breathing, all tiny and curled up in his daddy hand, his eyes all closed and them pretty lashes of his all pressed against his face.

Peanut ain't know it, but I started liking him right then. I wasn't even thinking nothing about doing it with him. I just liked the way his face looked when he was telling me the story. All soft and open.

I got his phone number and that night we started talking on the phone. I ain't give him my phone number, because Mama got our number unpublished and don't like me to be giving it out. Eboni the only one I give it to, and Mama ain't so crazy about even her having it. Peanut give me his number and I called him sometimes after I put Imani down.

Even though we ain't got no real classes together, that big head boy all the time want me to help him with his homework. I'm taking physical science. I don't know what kind of science Peanut taking, but they be doing mostly ditto sheets. One time they had a sheet about the parts of the flower and had to fill in the blanks. He say, The seed-bearing reproductive organ of a flower. That's the stamen, ain't it?

Which was wrong. Way wrong. It's the pistil, I say.

He say he was looking right at the picture and it ain't look like a pistol to him.

Not no gun, I say. A pis-til.

Oh, he say. Then he ask, What's a anther?

But I wouldn't tell him, because I could hear that he was playing his Nintendo, kicking and punching and shooting. I ask Peanut if he had a video game going, and he say he did.

He say he be home by hisself most of the time. His parents both work at the Freezer Queen three to eleven. He say his mama used to work seven to three, but his daddy say he never saw her, so they got on the same shift. Peanut say now he don't hardly see them. His daddy sometimes even get another shift at night to help Peanut sister out with her college money.

Peanut say he going to college on a basketball scholarship. Then it's on to the pros. I almost laughed. Not to be making fun of him or nothing. But Peanut just so little. He say he going to have big money when he go pro. He ain't got to do homework really, he say. Who in the NBA can tell you what a pistol is? he ask me. Peanut say he just want to talk to me, is all. He say he don't like being home by hisself. Reuben work in his daddy store after school, and Kente got to keep his little brothers while his mama at work. So they can't come over. Can you come over? he ask me.

I hadn't told him about Imani yet. I ain't know how he'd feel about me if he knew I have a baby, even though I was kind of thinking somebody might have told him already. I just told him I couldn't come.

Don't you like me? he ask.

I was real quiet on the phone just then. Just breathing into it. Peanut had turned off the video game.

I like you, he say.

No, you don't, I say. I'm fat.

No, you ain't, Peanut say. You big. Thick. My mama like that. That's the way I like girls to be.

I start laughing.

What's so funny? Peanut say. I'm for real.

The next day while we was eating lunch at school, I told Peanut about Imani. I told him in person so I could see his face. He act like he ain't know. He say, Get out of here, and wave his hand at me. You ain't got a baby. Maybe Peanut should be a actor and not no athlete. I ask him if that big-mouth Kente or somebody else had done told him already. Then he admitted that he heard it. I showed him Imani picture, and he say she was pretty. He say she look just like me.

Before I'd even go to Peanut house, I wanted him to meet Imani, so he went with me one day to get her from daycare. You should of seen Imani with him. She went right to him like she knew him and let him hold her while I was dressing her to go home. Imani let Peanut hold her on the bus, and he say, Maybe people think this my baby.

I told him they'd be thinking wrong because Imani mine and all mine.

Peanut want for us to come to his house that day. Your mama expect you home right now?

I told him Mama don't say nothing if I'm home by about six-thirty. My school bus pass run out at six, and if I get a bus right around then, I be home by six-thirty.

I usually stay over Eboni's until then, because sometimes Imani cry when I take her home. She be all tired and won't go to sleep no matter what I do or say, and then Mama start fussing. Not mean like, but telling me what to do. Feed her. Give her a bottle. Change her diaper. What she mostly say is put her down and let her cry herself out. Mama think I spoil Imani anyhow, hold her too much. But she my baby, and no matter what, Mama can't really tell me what to do.

At Eboni's, Miss Lovey don't fuss at me if Imani cry. Miss Lovey got two state kids, so I guess she used to children crying. Sometimes she come back in Eboni room where we be at and take Imani on up front with her. Then later I tell Eboni I got to go to the bathroom and sneak and watch Miss Lovey with a state baby on one shoulder and Imani laying across her lap. Miss Lovey be patting the state baby and just a shaking Imani on her knees. My baby be whining and fake crying. There ain't no way she going to escape Miss Lovey lap, and after a while it seem like she just give up and fall asleep.

If I wasn't going to Eboni that day, I sure wasn't going over to Peanut. I had a science test to study for. Peanut say he had the same test but wasn't studying.

I told him, Right, you getting a athlete's scholarship. You ain't got to study.

Not much, he say. Then he come up real close to me and kissed me right in the mouth. He let his hand real smooth slide down over one of my titties. I was going to brush it away, but I liked the way it made me feel. Like I was tingling inside. Even in my private parts. Peanut turned off real quick and headed down his block and I headed down mine in a hurry. I got to thinking this the same way Miss Odetta come home. She get off the bus right here. If she seen me, she going to tell Mama. I looked around for her, but she wasn't nowhere around.

It was something like a whole month before we was doing it. This the thing; I thought I would be too scared to. But Peanut the one make me not scared, even though I think he was.

We would go down to the family room in the basement. That's where we still go. To me it look like it's filled with all the broke-down furniture that lost its chance to be seen upstairs. There's a chair with a busted bottom, a table with water rings on it, a lamp with a hole in the shade. This big plaid couch with squashed-out cushions.

Peanut go on a killing spree playing his video games while I put Imani to sleep the way Miss Lovey do. I don't want her awake and looking at me. I put her in her stroller, and me and Peanut lay down on the couch and kiss with the lights out. That's all we did at first. I even let him kiss my titties, but I wouldn't take off my bra. I still don't. I done told him my titties ugly. They got stretch marks. He say he don't care. He just want to hold them naked in his hands, and I laugh.

When he put his tongue in my mouth, he be making these soft noises. His kisses just kept getting better and better to me.

Where he learn to kiss so good? I ask.

He say he just born good at it. He a natural born lover.

I don't know. Maybe he is. Maybe he was born knowing how to make them noises he making when we kiss. It's like he saying something to me. Something that go all inside me to the place in me I hardly know. He be making me want to know it. Peanut be finding a way to go in it and say things I hear deep inside me.

I don't be scared of him. He ain't never hurt me. Not even the first time. Peanut always be soft with me. He be fast, too. Like he the one scared. All the while when we be doing it, I be holding him close and listening to the place inside me and I don't be scared. I be listening so hard while Peanut making them noises in me, I don't be wanting him to stop.

Not even that first time. I ain't want him to stop. I only pulled down my panties and sweats to my knees. My stomach was all tight, and my legs was open just enough for him to do it. His eyelashes was tickling my face and he was steady kissing me. Making them sounds in my mouth, and every time he moved I sunk down deeper in that couch. Deeper and deeper. Listening to him somehow inside. I started crying. Peanut was done by then. It was like a minute. Maybe two. Anyway, it was real quick.

He switched on the light to see my face, and he ask, What's wrong? I ain't hurt you did I, Tasha?

No, I say him. You ain't hurt me at all.

Then why you crying?

I don't know, I say. I'm all right. I'm going to be all right.

I can't say I love Peanut. He don't never say he love me, and I don't never say I love him. I don't know. Love is something bigger. I do know I love Imani and Mama. I even love Eboni. Peanut. I don't know. He don't hurt me. And who know, maybe that's some kind of love.

THREE

My Mama, Your Mama

I BEEN INSIDE ME to the place I ain't never wanted to know. That's what I was thinking to tell Bett-Bett when she asked me why I wasn't in school this past week. I say to her I been sick. Which is good enough for her to know about my business. I don't need her digging up some bone and passing it around. Last thing she need to know is the truth. That I missed school because of *him*.

I ain't saying his name. I ain't never, ever going to say it. I won't ever put it in my mouth. I don't even want it in my mind, because it's all connected to his face. And the day I seen his face in the cafeteria three weeks ago, I thought I was going to die right there, holding a tray of tacos and fruit cocktail. I seen him coming right at me from the snack line where you pay with money, not lunch tickets. He had a whole tray of fries and he ain't even see me. But I seen him and dropped my tray on the floor and run out the cafeteria. I ain't stop running until I got to the lavatory, even though this security guard started chasing me, screaming, Where you think you going? What you done did?

But he couldn't come in the lavatory. Wasn't nothing but

these girls in there combing they heads and looking at theyselves in the mirror. I went in a stall and locked the door and I had to shit real bad. I usually can't go in a public place, but I couldn't hold it and I even sat down on the seat. Then this lady security guard come banging on the door of the stall I was in. Who in there? she ask.

I say, I'm sick. Can you just leave me alone? I ain't done nothing. I'm sick, is all.

She sick, I hear one them girls say. Hell, she smell like she dying. Then they laughed and I heard them leave. I was so embarrassed.

The security say, What you was running for? You know you ain't supposed to be running in the building.

And I'm thinking, Why she standing out there smelling my shit and asking me stupid questions? But I just say, I had to go.

She say, All right. I'll let you off this time. Next time you getting detention.

Then she left, too, and it was just me there with that boy name inside my head. With that boy name inside my mouth so nasty-tasting that I hocked and spit right on the floor. My knees was shaking like before. Like then. That night. I wished Eboni was with me but she ain't even in school now. She having two twins and her doctor say she need to be home in bed. She already know they girls, and she done picked out names. Asia and Aisha. I wanted to cry but it seem like my tears is all dried up in me and they left some craziness behind like salt. I could taste it in my mouth when I spit.

All I could think to do was get out of school, and I went right straight to the nurse to get me a excuse. The nurse a white man here at Lincoln. Who ever heard of a man a nurse? He act like he ain't want to let me go home.

I'm sick, I say.

Is that so? he say. He was reading a book and snapping gum like a girl. Then he ask, What time does your soap opera come on, girl? One or two?

I say, Excuse me. I'm for real. It's my stomach. I got my period and I got some bad cramps. I done bled through three straight pads this morning.

He looked at me like he done heard that excuse a thousand times before and say, I don't care if you go home or not. It's no skin off my nose, hon.

Static. Static. Static. That's the thing be getting to me about school. Elementary school. Middle school. High school. Ain't no difference. It's all the time some teacher nem act like they know you. Act like they can shine a light inside your head and see what you thinking.

I ain't say nothing to that nurse. I let him think that my head was so empty that all I want to do was fill it watching some stupid-ass soaps about a bunch of skinny white women wearing expensive clothes and living in fancy houses even if they supposed to be poor and having a bunch of make-believe problems. Black women too. They lives be just like the white women's. Fake. I got real problems. So I kept my mouth all shut up and got my excuse.

Then I got Imani from the nursery. She was sleeping, looking just like *me*. Even though I can't say I know what I really look like when I sleep, because I be sleeping and can't see myself. But it's got to be just like Imani. My eyes shut real tight like I'm studying on something. Like there be something in my dreams I especially want to see.

Mrs. Poole say babies dream. She say don't nobody know what they dream about. Sometime Imani be laughing in her sleep. If it's night, she be waking me up. I jump up thinking that girl wake. But she ain't, and I stand over her crib looking at her. I know Imani got to be dreaming about something. I be hoping it's me. Wishing there was a way I could climb down inside her dream and shine a light on me holding her in my arms. Seeing me rocking her in my arms strong like the branches of the tree outside my bedroom window. And her laughing because I'm rocking her higher and higher, past all the soft leaves and into the dark where the moon rising over us and she know she safe because I'm holding her and won't never ever let her fall.

When I was little, sometime I would wake up laughing. I never could remember exactly about what. I like to think it was Mama and me I was laughing about. That she was holding me with love all in her arms.

There wasn't no way I was going home that time of day. Mama would just have some more static for me, so I went over to Eboni. Miss Lovey wasn't there. Eboni was, and she wasn't even in bed like she was supposed to be. She was in the kitchen, making Buffalo wings. Her school tutor was already gone for the day. She ask me, Girl, what's the matter?

I was wondering if I looked so bad. If I looked so crazy. If that boy name was wrote right across my face. I say, I had to cut out early because I wasn't feeling good. Eboni know me real good. I know she could tell that wasn't all. But she say, Have lunch with me.

Imani was still sleep and I put her down in Eboni room and finished up making the chicken while Eboni sat down. I told her, You know you shouldn't even be on your feet.

Eboni say, Shoot, I'm hungry and I'm eating for three people.

I say, You should have wait until your mama come home. Miss Lovey a good cook.

Eboni say, She don't cook like I want. The doctor got me off salt and I ain't supposed to be eating fried foods. I done gained seventy-five pounds.

I ain't say nothing to Eboni about her weight. Because it wouldn't be nothing but the pot calling the kettle black. I'd already dumped almost a half block of some government butter in the skillet to melt over the wings. I got the hot sauce and had poured on a half of a big bottle, and Eboni say, Put on more.

You crazy, I say. They hot enough and that sauce full of salt.

She say, Then add some cayenne.

I put in a whole heap and Eboni took the plate of wings I fixed up for her with blue cheese and celery. She was eating them wings and slinging bones like she was starving. I sat there all quiet like, just watching the pile of empty bones grow on her plate.

She say, I know something really wrong with you if you ain't eating nothing. What happened at school?

I seen him, I say with my voice as flat as I could make it, trying to sound like I was feeling real normal and had some sense. Like the craziness ain't take me all over.

Who? Peanut? she ask.

I say, Not no Peanut. I don't care nothing about no Peanut. I seen *him*. You know who I mean. For a few seconds I think Eboni didn't know who I was talking about until she looked at me real hard in the face and I just know she seen that boy name wrote there.

Oooh, she say, sucking grease off her fingers. No, you ain't even seen *him*.

I did, I say. Right in the cafeteria. I guess he been there all the time. Ain't no way I would've ever come to Lincoln if I know that's where he go.

Eboni say, You should transfer. When I have the twins, I ain't coming back to Lincoln. I'm going to East. It's closer. Come with me.

Soon as Eboni say that, I got a pain right in my stomach like I needed to go to the bathroom again. I was thinking, How I'm going to tell Mama I want to switch schools? If I ain't want to after the shooting last month, ain't no way she was going to believe I want to do it now.

Lincoln ain't that kind of school where there be shootings and stabbings like it's a regular way of life. It ain't locked down like a prison and you got to be passing through metal detectors and getting patted down. Wasn't never even no shooting there until that day.

We was just being dismissed. I had got Imani from the nursery and had her in her stroller. We was in the main hall, where there was like two hundred to three hundred kids, when all these other kids come busting back in the main doors, running and screaming. They shooting. They shooting outside, they was screaming. And they kept on running right up the hall, pushing past people. Teachers. Kids. They even knocked down a security guard. Then all the kids already in the hall started running. I swear my heart wasn't even beating I was so scared. I thought they was going to run right over me and Imani. I snatched my baby out her stroller. Her leg got caught in the strap. I jerked her hard and got her loose just as I got smashed into some lockers. But I bounced off. I ain't have to think about where to go. The crowd carried me into the front office, where the principal and secretaries nem be. I got pushed behind the main desk where the secretaries was already on the floor. Everybody kept on pushing and screaming and I almost fell. Then I heard the principal, Mr. Diaz, yelling for us to all lay down. Get down, he say. Get down. Stay down!

I fell right where I was and landed on some girl who ain't say nothing. Then this boy landed right on top of me and Imani. And Imani started screaming. My baby, I say. You squashing my baby. Get off!

He was crying. Big old boy too, with hair on his face. I wasn't crying. But I could feel my heart then going like crazy. Imani wasn't hurt. She was scared. Her eyes was all big like she want me to tell her what was going on. But I ain't know. I just held her tight to me.

Mr. Diaz jumped over the main desk like he was Superman or something. One of the secretaries was screaming, Mr. Diaz don't go out there. But he kept right on going. I could hear him in the halls telling kids to get down.

I ain't hear no gunshots. But all I could think was somebody was dead right outside the school and if I'd stepped out them doors a few minutes earlier it could've been me or Imani. Or whoever was shooting could run right on in the building and kill us where we was laying. I started shaking then. Thinking, Who would ever want to die like this? On some regular old schoolday. At some regular old school laying under a desk too scared to move. I wanted to go home.

Mr. Diaz come back in a few minutes and say for us all to return to homeroom. Don't go out the building until I say to. After the police come. Then he got on the intercom. Saying for everybody to stay calm and if they was hurt, to come to the nurse office.

I was still shaking when I left the office. The halls was

packed and some kids was crying and others was laughing. These boys was saying that some dude got shot in the butt, that was all. They was laughing and other kids was laughing. Even some who was crying started laughing. Books and papers and backpacks everywhere. There was sneakers laying right where kids had run out of them. Half of the lockers open. I seen my stroller. It wasn't bad off. It was real dirty where it got stepped on, and one of the arms was bent, but I could still push it.

Me and Mama and Miss Odetta watched the news that night, and the shooting was on every channel. The boy was really only shot in the butt and they didn't keep him at the hospital. They say his wound was superficial. Mr. Diaz come on the news, looking all smooth. Like nothing happened. He say our school a good school and they ain't never had no problem like this. The boy that was shot didn't go to our school. It's outside agitators. All the while he saying this, some kids was jumping up and down in the background and making faces, laughing. Then they interviewed this girl and boy who say they seen a jeep. It started going slow and pulled up in front of a bus. Then *pow pow pow pow pow*. Like it's the Wild Wild West. That's all they seen, because they ran back inside. The newsman say it's a miracle nobody else got hurt or killed.

Miss Odetta say, They ain't going to catch nobody. You wait and see.

Mama say, Ain't this some shit? In front a school. They could've killed a bunch of kids. Them the kind of niggers don't care about nobody. I'm telling you. You ain't safe no goddamn place no more.

I say, They was probably all some drug dealers coming by our school messing things up.

Miss Odetta say, That ain't got to be true. Why it got to be about drugs? She pulled a cigarette out her bra and lighted it. Then she say, Shit. Niggers was getting shot before there ever was drug dealers.

Mama give me a look and smile behind Miss Odetta back. Me and her knew not to say nothing else. We know Miss Odetta just say that because of June Bug. Miss Odetta know we know that June Bug dealing. Miss Odetta the one act like what he do is all right. Living on the down low in her basement. You can't say nothing having to do with drugs without Miss Odetta throwing her two cent in. And what I really want to be doing when she do is throw her back a penny in change.

Mama say, They need to catch them and throw they asses under the jail.

Miss Odetta say, Don't hold your breath.

Mama asked if I want to go to another school. I told her I didn't. I got my daycare and everything all set up at Lincoln.

Mr. Diaz had a assembly the next day to tell us everything was safe. Even though I was thinking he can't stop some fool from shooting. I mean, damn, if he can do that, he need to come around my way. Because they still be shooting around here. If there's some shooting when me and Imani is up late, she don't look at me like she done the first time she heard it. Like she got a question. Seem like she done already figured out the answer.

So things just settled back down to regular at Lincoln. The only trouble was that mess girls keep going. There some jealous girls go to our school. A group of bitches who roam in packs. They don't like you if you pretty, so I don't have no problems with them. They don't even see me. They hunt girls like Coco. Two of them bitches beat Coco up in a lavatory. Ain't no way skinny little Coco stand a chance against no two girls. They ripped five extensions out her head right from the root. Tore her shirt and bra right off her. Scratched up her face. Coco say they told her she wasn't nothing. She wasn't shit. Coco ain't tell who it was. She too scared.

I know how she feel about not telling. Even though she know who them girls is. She got to see them every day. But she keep right on going like they ain't even there. With a secret. Ever since she was jumped, Coco carry a knife. Not no little one neither. She showed it to me. It's a butcher knife like your mama keep in the kitchen drawer and be chopping on meat with. She have it right in her backpack inside one of her notebooks. She keep the pack half zipped so she can get to it easy.

He say he had a knife. That night. He ain't never show it to me. He say if he had to show it to me, he was going to have to use it on me. So he kept it like a secret.

When I was talking to Eboni that day after I seen him at school, I was thinking maybe that was what I need. A secret to keep me safe. Maybe I could sneak a knife out the house without Mama knowing, or go down to the Woolworth and buy one down in they basement. I'd be like Coco, have it where I could get to it easy. If he was to say something to me, he'd know all about it. I'd stab his ass right in the broad daylight in the cafeteria. But that was just that dried-up craziness in me. There ain't no way I could do something like that. Not having Imani. I don't know what she'd do if I was took from her or she was took from me.

Greasing on her chicken wings Eboni say to me, You

should do like you should of done in the first place, Tasha. Tell your mama.

I got me another pain in my stomach. I say, My mama ain't your mama. If Miss Lovey was my mama, I would've told her straight off.

Eboni say, *My mother. Your mother. Live across the way. Fifteen. Sixteen. East Broadway.* It was a song we'd sing when we was picking sides for kickball. We'd be lining ourselves up so we could end up on the same side. Eboni knew I'd give her the next lines of the song. *Every night they have a fight and this is what they say. Icka Bicka Backa Soda Cracker. Out. Go. She.* We finished up together.

But I say to her, I'm for real, Eboni. You know I can't tell my mama. And don't you be even telling Miss Lovey. Eboni was sucking on a bone and making no promises to me.

When Imani woke up, I took her on home. It was still light out. Before I unlocked the front door, I stood on the porch and erased my face. I closed my eyes and wrote on it that I just come from another boring day of school, because I knew the first thing I would see was Mama sitting on the couch looking me dead in the mouth when I walked in. But she wasn't sitting there. The house ain't had no smell like some dinner had been cooking, neither. It smelled like perfume. I knew right then Mama was going out.

She done met some man I ain't even seen yet. He call sometime. All he say is can he speak to Earlene. Then she take the call up in her room. The thing is, he been calling for over a month and ain't never been to our house. Mama meet him off somewhere. That make me think he ain't got no car. Or she don't want me meeting him.

I went upstairs with Imani and peeked in Mama room. It was a mess. Her dresser top was covered with all kinds of makeup and brushes and sponges. Her shoes was all in a heap on the floor, and it looked like she threw all her outfits across her bed. All it seem she decided on to wear was her nice bra and drawers. The kind men be liking. All black and made from lace.

Mama was sitting on the end of the bed with her face all made up, looking all pretty and soft, putting lotion on her legs. Her body all skinny like she ain't never had a baby. Even her stomach flat. It got only a few thin stretch marks that circle her belly button like the petals on a flower. They so tiny you can't hardly even see them. It's like I was in her but barely left no sign I was there.

She say, Come on in here, Tasha.

I could only get the door part open. I squeezed in with Imani on my hip.

Mama say, I was fenna to leave you a note. But you here now. I'm going out. There's a food stamp on the kitchen table if you want to go up to the Arabian store and get yourself something for dinner.

I ask, Where you going, Mama?

She say, Out. And smile like a girl going on a date. I don't know. Maybe she feel like a girl. Mama ain't nothing but thirty-two.

I ask, Well, when you coming back?

When I feel like it, Mama say. Girl, I'm grown. I know my way home. Why you in my business? Do I be in your business?

I say, Yeah, Mama, you do be.

And Mama laugh and snap the bottle of lotion shut. You

damn straight I be in your business. Because I'm the mama and you the child. It's my job to know your business. Did you take your pill today, Tasha?

I say, I did. I always take it, Mama. You going out with Royster? I ask. Even though I know it ain't been him calling. Mama busted out laughing, and me too. Even Imani laughed like she knew who we was talking about.

Child, Mama say, I ain't even going out with the Jherri Curl King no more.

Mama was dating Royster before Imani was born. I never did like him. Royster old enough to be Mama daddy. He all the time had a plastic bag on his head that stuck to his bald spot in the middle. Mostly I ain't like him because he married. What Mama want with a married man, I don't know. Miss Odetta got her this married man Simpkin she been going out with ever since I can remember. He give Miss Odetta money. Maybe Mama thought Royster going to give her money. But he never gave her none I ever seen.

Mama got up from the bed and I sat down behind her with Imani. Imani started squirming and whining to get down. I ain't want to let her down in all that mess. She wasn't going to do nothing but put something in her mouth. These days she be putting all kinds of things in her mouth she find on the floor. I bounced her on my lap. Imani liked that.

Mama say, If you go up to the store, get some more bread. She was pulling on a pair of tight jeans.

I say, I don't think I'm going. I don't feel so good.

Mama put on a red blouse and left the top three buttons open. Then she come over to me, kicking shoes out the way. She put the back of her hand to my head. It was all cool, and I smelled her perfume sweet like some candy. I could see right down her shirt to her titties.

Mama say, You cool as a cucumber, girl.

I say, It's my stomach.

Mama say, Tasha, you just need to sit on the toilet. You probably constipated. Seem like you trying to get me to stay home with you tonight like you some baby.

I ain't say nothing. I looked at Imani. She got hold of Mama housedress and was chewing on a button. Mama went over to the mirror, brushing her hair. I did want Mama to stay home. But I ain't want to say it.

Mama say, Miss Odetta right next door if you need something. She was still looking in the mirror.

Imani need changing, I say. When I took the button out her mouth, she start crying, so I knew it was time for me to leave. I went to my room. Maybe I *was* being a baby. But I ain't want to see Mama go out. I turned my radio up all loud so I wouldn't have to hear the front door shut.

That evening I went on with the routine of feeding Imani and getting her ready for bed. When I put her in the tub, she kept on saying, Dada. Dada. She been saying that for a while now, but when she say it that night, it made me think of *him*. I washed off her tongue with the washcloth. Trying to wash that word right out her mouth. Don't you be saying that, I say. You say Mama. Mama.

Imani wasn't even stutting me. She kept right on saying Dada like she been saying. When I went to wipe out her mouth again, she grabbed hold of the rag and sucked on it like it was a bottle. My baby probably thought I was crazy. Which I ain't. I was just on my way.

She went right to sleep after I give her a bottle, so I ain't had no excuse for not doing homework. I left Imani in her crib, went on downstairs, and turned on the TV. I had a Latin test coming up on Friday. But I couldn't even keep my mind on my work. I wanted to talk to somebody. I thought about calling Eboni. But she had already told me what she thought I should do. So I picked up the phone and called Peanut. I ain't even let it ring one whole time before I hung up. I knew he ain't want me calling him.

Like the nut he is, Peanut done left Lincoln. He transferred to South Park High. We don't mess around no more. I don't know. I think he done changed. He act like he don't want to be with me now. Maybe he sick of doing it with me. If I call him, he act like I'm bothering him. He always got some excuse to get off the phone real quick. He tired. He on the other line. He doing homework. Like he do homework! He made the basketball team there. J.V. He say that keep him busy. But I know he ain't just getting busy with no basketball. I know he seeing another girl.

Coco the one brung me that bone. Her cousin go to South Park too, and Coco say her cousin say Peanut be with this mixed girl. He be kissing her on the bus. It's not like I love him or nothing. I miss being with Peanut. Kissing him. I don't really miss doing it with him. He do it so fast. I always just wanted to get back to the kissing. I be dreaming about him sometime. That his long eyelashes is tickling my neck and I wake up laughing, and then be mad because it was only a dream.

It seem like after you been with somebody, after they done been all up inside you, that you could call them up. That you could say anything to them. Like, Hey, there's something that's bothering me. I don't want you to do nothing but listen to me talk. To let me get this boy name out my mind. To get his name out my mouth. Off my face. You think a person could do that. But I ain't even try it with Peanut. If I would've called him up and he had rushed me off the phone like I wasn't nothing to him. Like he was so great and I was just some stupid bitch he was throwing table scraps to by actually talking to me for two minutes on the phone. I would've gone all the way to crazy.

I ain't had nobody to talk to. I couldn't tell Mama about him. I couldn't tell her about that night. How stupid I was that night, the summer before Imani was born. Thinking he really liked me. As fat as I am. As black as I am. As much as my body look like it ain't never supposed to be loved by no boy. Touched by no boy. That's why I went from Skate-A-Rama with him instead of staying there like I should have. Because he say he liked me! I was smiling back too. Eboni wasn't there, because she was home on punishment. I wasn't skating much, because I'd rented a smaller size skate than what I really take. I was wearing a nine then, and I ain't want that big red number blazing out from the back of my skate, telling the world how big my feet was. So I got me a size seven. They was real cute on my feet while I was sitting down on a bench looking at them. He come up to me while I was sitting down judging my feet. He ain't even have on no skates. He ain't say nothing at first. Just sat there. I pretended like I was watching everybody skate so I could sneak a look at him. I can't say he looked fine to me. Because he didn't. He was big. Bigger than me and he had good hair. It wasn't no curl neither he was trying to fake up to look like good hair. His hair wasn't at all greasy, and he had it just long enough so you could see it had a natural curl to it. When I turned my head away, he say something to me. I ain't hear what he say because the music was so loud. So he slid up next to me and screamed loud in my ear his name. He ask me my name and I told him. The music was so loud, I couldn't hardly hear nothing he say. I did hear his name real clear and I heard him say he like me. We ended up going outside, because it was too loud to talk in there.

I turned in my skates and got my hand stamped so I could come back inside. You can't get no skates again, the lady behind the counter say. This session end in a half hour. You done for the night. I told her that was all right. Then I went out with him. Just to the parking lot, where we can talk, he say. There was some kids hanging out there. They was talking all loud. I wasn't stutting them. But he took hold of my hand and kept on walking. Where we going? I ask. Around the back, he say. Where it's more quieter. We can talk back there. You ain't scared of the dark, is you? No, I say. I ain't scared of no dark. And me, like a stupid stupid fool, walked right on with him. Like we was some couple just walking in love. I wasn't really thinking about no love with him. I was thinking about him saying, I like you, Tasha. Like he mean it. Like I was someone special to him. Like I was someone special to somebody even if it was a lie.

It was cool out even though it was August. Soon as we went around back, I could smell him. I don't know why I ain't smell him inside. But out in the dark quiet he smelled like smoke. Me and him went up this little hill into these trees and he took off his jacket for me to sit on. I don't even remember what we talked about, because we only talked a couple minutes. I know he never did say again that he liked me. I would've remembered that. He never said I was pretty or nothing before he kissed me right in the mouth. It wasn't like

I never kissed a boy before. I did kiss this Puerto Rican boy two times around Eboni house and let him touch me outside my clothes. But when he was kissing me that night, I ain't like it. His mouth tasted real nasty. I tasted dirt before, when I was little, and his mouth tasted worse than dirt. I guess his mouth was like that from smoking. Like some nasty little animal had done crawled inside his mouth and built a nest.

All the while he steady kissing me and I'm steady trying not to breathe. Trying not to swallow so I wouldn't taste him while he was laying me back to the cold ground. I pulled my mouth away and say, Get on up off me. I don't know what you trying to do.

He say, What you want me to do. And he steady pushing me down harder. I could feel it then. His thing. It was pressing up inside my legs. All hard and mad inside his jeans. I tried to sit up. But he pressed his whole weight on me, squashing my titties so hard they hurt.

Hey, I screamed, leave me alone! Get up off of me! He put one of his big hands across my nose and mouth. I was screaming and kicking and trying to peel his hand off. But my screams wasn't doing no good. They was so tiny they never even escaped the trees. That's all I could hear, even though that boy talking to me real low with his face right in mine.

I don't know how many times he say, I got a knife. I got a knife. Before I heard it. But when I heard that, I stopped trying to scream. I stopped trying to fight.

Then he say, If I got to show it to you, I'm going to have to use it on you. Now shut up, you fat bitch, and take down your fucking pants. I had already shut up. He took his hand off my face and raised up off of me some. But I ain't move. So he pulled at my sweat pants. That's when I started helping him, because I was thinking he going to tear them, and how was I going to explain that to Mama?

It was the both of us that got them halfway down when he say for me to turn over and get on my knees. He raised up some more to let me turn over and I could see the lights of the Skate-A-Rama coming through the tops of the trees. When I turned over, he pushed my head down to the ground and I couldn't see nothing no more. I ain't hear nothing until he pushed his naked self up against me and started doing it. And my hands grabbed for something to hold.

Hanging on to the grass, I swear I could hear them screams of mine quieter and quieter sinking into the ground. All the time I'm thinking, This ain't real. This got to be a dream. Not my dream. His dream. He done thought this all up in his mind. Had this all up in his mind. When I was thinking about him liking me, he was thinking about this. I'm all embarrassed with my butt all tooted up in the air and him sticking his thing in me harder and harder. Faster and faster. It seem like to me his thing was a knife. Mad with me. Cutting me. My insides was burning a little bit more. A little bit more. A little bit more. I couldn't stop my knees from shaking, and I was holding my breath in me to stop the pain.

He put his face right up next to mine and his breath come right in my ear. It was so strong I could taste it in my mouth. You know you like it, you stupid cunt, he say. Tell me you like it. Tell me to fuck you some more.

I ain't say nothing. He grabbed me by the hair. My breath come out in a moan.

He say, Yeah, that's right. That's right. He pushed my face back to the ground and got up off me. You can tell anybody you want, he say. I don't give a goddamn. Ain't nobody going to believe your dumb ass no way. He yanked his jacket up from under me. I heard him take off out them trees.

It was a while before I even moved. I don't know how long I stayed just like he left me, still burning inside. When I figured he was gone, really gone, I rolled over on my side and touched myself quick down there to see if I was bleeding. I was all wet. I ain't know if it was blood. The night was so dark, even with the yellow lights shining above me in the leaves. So I pulled my pants up and brushed myself off. My knees wouldn't stop shaking. But I got up. I ain't even went back in the Skate-A-Rama. I ain't even went back through the parking lot the way I came. I was shamed. I went around the other side and waited for the bus home. Spitting. Spitting. Spitting all the time I was waiting.

Mama was sitting on the couch when I got home. Watching TV with the lights out. She ain't even look up when I come in. It was a Friday night and she like to watch a cop show that come on. Mama say, Lock the door behind you. Which I did, and went right straight upstairs into the bathroom and pulled down my pants and panties. There wasn't no whole bunch of blood like I was expecting to see. Only a little spot, already turning dark like a old penny. That made me feel better. Like things wasn't so bad. Like I wasn't going to have to tell Mama about it because it was just a bad dream anyway.

I took me a shower and brushed my teeth with the water running all over me. I kept brushing them and brushing them, squirting out long white worms of toothpaste until my mouth tasted fresh and clean like mouths be on commercials. Like mint. Then I washed myself. I ain't even want to touch myself down there in my private parts. But I squatted down, with my knees still shaking, and washed off real gentle but real good two times. I wasn't burning like I was before.

When I laid down in bed that night, with the moon shining through the tree outside my window, with the moon shining down on me, I wanted to get up and go downstairs and tell Mama. I should have told her right then. I was so shamed. Even though my mouth was clean, seem like when I just thought of that boy, I got that nasty taste in my mouth again, and I wiped off my tongue with the back of my hand. I ain't want Mama to think it was me that was the nasty one. But I wanted her to come to me in my room that night because I was quiet. Because I had come in and gone straight upstairs. Which I never did. Showered without being told and got right into bed with no radio playing. No light on. No nothing. How come Mama ain't know that wasn't even me acting like that? What was she thinking about if she wasn't thinking about me? Royster, the Jherri Curl King?

When I was a little girl, if I was out of her sight and quiet for a minute, it seem like Mama would come to me. I would look up to see her face over me. Full and shining like the moon. Mama would watch me until she was satisfied I was all right and then she would slip away quiet. Quiet as the setting of the moon. I wouldn't even know she was gone until I looked up and seen she wasn't there.

I hid in the dark of my room that night like I was some little girl too shamed to tell on myself for doing something so stupid. Mama always been the one thinking I'm so smart. I'm so special. That I'm the one who has got a brain that's going to take me somewhere in my life. Maybe Mama think I got a brain that will take her somewhere too one day. Put her in a fine house. But that night I wasn't none of the things Mama say about me. I was what *he* say I was. All them nasty words he called me. Words Mama never would let me put in my mouth to say. *Fat bitch. Stupid cunt.* How I was going to open my mouth and say them words? Just thinking about them set me off crying. Not like I was crazy. I ain't make nam sound. And why ain't Mama come? She could've pushed the door to my room open and when the light of the hall fell on me she would've seen my face. Telling her what my two lips couldn't.

But Mama ain't come to me that night, and after then it was just easier to keep my mouth shut and let Mama think I was good and not nasty. So I opened up this place inside to leave everything he done and said to me. Not like it never happened. Because it did happen. But I found a place where I could close it off, and I really did think like some child, like some girl, like some fool, I wasn't never going to have to go inside it again.

After seeing *him* in the cafeteria, I knew that wasn't true. No matter how it looked to anybody, for the next two days after I seen him, I went back to that place. I was in it each night, curled up inside like some big old baby waiting to be born.

Instead of going to school, I went to Eboni's. Miss Lovey was home, looking after her state kids. She ain't say nothing to me about nothing when me and Imani went back in Eboni room and stayed until the tutor left. She ain't ask why I was there. I knew Eboni had told her. But I knew she wouldn't say nothing to my mama. Out in the kitchen, she made me one of her big meals. I could smell a chicken baking, greens boiling away with vinegar and hot pepper. Yams roasting with they sweet juice dripping in the stove. My stomach was making all kinds of noise just smelling how good that food was going to taste. But when it came time to eat it, I really ain't had no appetite.

I sat down with Eboni and Miss Lovey and them state kids in the kitchen. Miss Lovey made her and the oldest state kid a plate. He about three and he don't eat so much. His mama was on crack when she had him. Miss Lovey get WIC and food stamps. She be getting government cheese and butter, and he still so skinny he look like he could fall over if you blow on him. All he was eating was a teaspoon of food. Eboni, shoot, she was eating like food was going out of style at the end of the day. I ate me a plate just to be polite to Miss Lovey.

I went around Eboni house the next day, too, but on the third day Eboni wasn't there. Miss Lovey was all out of breath and sweating when she come to the door. She say, Come on in the kitchen. And I went. Miss Lovey was making grits and frying up some fish. She say, Eboni had her girls early this morning. I'm telling you, it was a easy labor. They were a minute apart. It seems like they were racing to get in the world. They're both healthy thank God and so pretty with good hair swirled around their heads. I say, Oooh, I want to go see her and the babies. Miss Lovey say, I'm sure Eboni wants to see you, too. You can leave Imani next door where I left the kids and we can go up to the hospital later. She made herself a plate and one for me.

I say, I ain't really hungry. I already ate.

Miss Lovey wasn't even stutting me. She opened up the stove and took out a pan of biscuits and put two on my plate. For a while she ain't say nothing. She ate. Sprinkling hot sauce on her fish. Slurping from a big cup of juice. Putting jelly and butter on her biscuits. I cracked open one of them hot biscuits and buttered and jellied it for Imani, who was sitting in her stroller whining because she knew there was food but wasn't none of it coming to her mouth. I fed some to her and tasted it for myself. It was good. I could tell it wasn't from no can popped open on the counter. Then I looked up at Miss Lovey and stopped eating. She had that I-know-you-got-a-secret look on her face. Right then I knew Eboni must have told.

You know, Miss Lovey say, I been meaning to talk to you.

I cut her right off. Not in a mean way. But I say, I know what you fenna say, Miss Lovey.

Miss Lovey say, Is that so? If you know what I'm going to say, you need to be on one of those psychic telephones making some money for yourself, child.

I bust out laughing, even though I ain't want to.

Miss Lovey put one of her hands on top of one of mines. It was warm and soft.

She say, Child, you have to go back to school. Shooting the hook won't solve your problems.

I say, I know that, Miss Lovey.

She say, You don't act like it. I know you're scared of that boy who raped you.

I looked down at the table. That was the first time that word been said.

Then Miss Lovey said it again. She say, I believe he did rape you.

I ain't say nothing. Miss Lovey reached over with her other hand and started rubbing my back. Round and round in circles like you rub a baby back to get them to sleep. Like I rub Imani. She say, It's all right to talk to me about it.

I couldn't say nothing. I just found my hand that was on

the table squeezing her hand tight tight. Miss Lovey ain't ask me to say nothing else. She moved up close to me and put my head down on her shoulder and kept rubbing my back with her hand all warm. Pulling me back from inside myself. She was pulling me back every time she made a circle. Made a circle. Made a circle. It was like she was looking for the place I was. Reaching down inside that cold dark with her warm hand. Picking me up from that ground. Pulling me out into the world where I opened my eyes into the soft light.

It was a while before I lifted up my face. When Imani saw it she started crying. Miss Lovey picked her up and put her on her lap to rock her. She fed some grits to Imani right off her plate. Miss Lovey say, Go back to Lincoln on Monday and see how you feel. If you want to get out, I'll help you.

I say, Only my mama can do that.

Miss Lovey say, I'll talk to your mother then.

I just shook my head.

Miss Lovey say, I won't tell her nothing you haven't. It's up to you to tell her about the rape. She needs to hear that from your lips. But you need to be in school. What kind of future can you make for this child with no education? I looked at my little greedy baby and she put out her arms to come to me and I took her in my arms. I was holding her all close feeling her heart beating up next to mines. Miss Lovey say for me not be worrying about going to another school. She say I would only have to cross that bridge if I come to it.

I made myself go back to Lincoln the next Monday. I was real nervous. About running into him. But I had so much schoolwork to catch up on, I spent most of my time with my mind on that. In the cafeteria I was looking for him and not looking for him, thinking maybe I wouldn't have to come to that bridge at all. It was the middle of the week before I seen him. Me and Coco was sitting together at lunch. I wasn't hardly eating. I was studying for a Latin test. When the bell rung we was rushing to take our trays up. That's when I seen him, just ahead of us at the dish room, putting his dirty tray on the belt. There I was at the bridge. I wasn't even thinking about crossing it. I wanted to jump off. Kids was pushing up behind me to take they trays back. My feet took on a mind of they own and ain't even move when he turned around to leave.

Coco stepped up right next to me and took my tray. What's wrong with you, Tasha? she asked. Making us late?

That boy looked up then. I got a pain in my stomach, thinking he heard my name. But he ain't even look at me. He was looking at Coco. Smiling at her. She sucked her teeth and rolled her eyes at him, and the smile he had on his face slid right off. He walked off without saying nothing.

I seen him the next day in the cafeteria, and he walked right on by me without noticing me. I knew I wasn't going to cross no bridge after all. I could feel it in my heart that he ain't know who I was. I was some girl with no name. I was some girl with no face. I was just some girl in a dream he ain't even remember.

FOUR

Ten Little Angels

I MIGHT have killed Imani. That's what I come to find out from Mrs. Poole right before our Christmas break. But I ain't know. How was I supposed to know?

Shaken Baby Syndrome. Mrs. Poole was talking about it in the class one day but I wasn't paying no good attention to her. I was looking at a magazine I had inside my notebook. *Seventeen*. It was a December one, full of ways to dazzle everybody at holiday parties. There was this white girl in a plaid dress that was red, green, and black that look like a tablecloth. She was at a party and there was some white boys with teeth like Chiclets and presents in they hands or standing under some mistletoe ready to get kissed. I imagined me at one of them parties in a velvet dress and fifty pounds skinnier with some braids Eboni put in. They tight and hurting my head, but I ain't care because they looked good. I ain't have on the earrings Eboni gave me, the ones with my name on them, because they say *projects*. They say East Side. Fruit Belt. Humboldt Parkway. Jefferson Avenue. You ride the 12 *and* 13 bus. They say all that with just your name spelled out in fake gold.

So I had on some pearl studs. Real tasteful. I looked so good, it's like I'm the belle of the ball like them white girls in the magazine. And then Mrs. Poole walked right in the party, talking about death.

Shaking a baby can cause its death, she say. Shaken Baby Syndrome. Never, Mrs. Poole say. Never shake your baby for no reason. Because you mad. Because they crying and working your nerves. Even because you just playing with them and throwing them up in the air.

I closed up my notebook with the magazine. Mrs. Poole was holding a bald naked baby doll, just a-shaking it. Some girls was laughing, because the doll big head was flopping around. Mrs. Poole stopped shaking it and say what would happen to a real baby. You could bounce they brain against the inside of they head and give them a concussion. That's a brain injury. She say you can shake a baby so hard, you can break they neck. Snap they spinal cord. That's how you can kill them. Everybody stopped laughing. You could hear the lights and clock humming and somebody screaming like a crazy person out in the hall.

I was looking at the doll all naked on the desk, wishing Eboni was there. I tried to remember if Mrs. Poole say something about this before. She make me sick, talking about stupid shit like routines and schedules and burping and how often to change a diaper, but ain't say nothing about not shaking a baby. Because I already done it.

I shook Imani just the week before. I ain't shake her because I was playing with her. I was shaking her because she be making me mad and get on my nerves. We was supposed to be going to a birthday party Bett-Bett was having for her youngest baby. Her son just turned one, and I had been pinching pennies so I could go and take Imani. It was at Party Time Pizza. I had to pay my own way in and get a gift. Mama say it's a waste of money to have a party for a baby so little. They don't remember it. But I wanted to go. So when Imani have her birthday, some other girls and babies will be there to make it a party.

Me and Imani ain't get to go, though. Imani was sick for two straight weeks before the party. At first she got the runs. I was changing her once a hour. Then she started throwing up and had a fever, so I took off from school to take her to ECMC. She see a pediatrician there. He a man from India with black black greasy hair and skin so pretty, it's like chocolate pudding. He say Imani was teething and she had a cold and a ear infection too. He say not to take her to no daycare. She should stay home a few days. So I had to stay home with Imani, and she doing nothing but crying and whining and rubbing her fist in her mouth and grabbing at her ears. Mama was sick of both of us by the second day. I was wishing she would just go off with her secret boyfriend, but she kept coming into my room, asking why Imani was crying so. What I was doing to her? I told her I wasn't doing nothing to her. She crying because she sick. Mama want to pour some warm olive oil in Imani ears. The doctor ain't say nothing about that, so I wouldn't let her do it. She ask if I put that teething gel on her gums. And I ain't lie about that. I told her I ain't put it on there because Imani bit me last time I tried. Mama laugh at me. That's part of being a mama, she say. Pain. Sometimes you got to do things to your children they don't like. Things that hurt them if it's good for them. I say, I ain't never going to hurt my child for nothing. Mama say, You don't know what the hell you talking about. Why you think you know so goddamn much? I say, Mrs. Poole teach us how to take care of a baby.

That was the wrong thing to say to Mama.

Mrs. Poole? Mama say. Mrs. Poole? Who is that cockeye bitch to teach you anything? What she know about babies, what she read in some book?

I want to say Mrs. Poole got four children, but instead I say, Mama, I know what I'm doing.

Mama say, If you know what you was doing, you wouldn't never have had no baby in the first place. Then she left me and Imani alone.

I was smoking mad with Mama. Saying I ain't know what I'm doing. Talking to me like I'm some fool! Imani was fussing. I sat with her on my bed and give her her teething ring. She bit it one time and threw it across the room. Her nose was all snotty, so I tried to suck out the snot with one of them little bulb things. She hated it and started screaming and kicking like I was abusing her, and I stopped. I started rocking her like Miss Lovey rock her, across my knees. I was jiggling and jiggling and she crying and crying. I turned on the radio. But she ain't shut up. So I started singing to Imani "Ten Little Angels." She stopped crying and only whined while I was singing, so I kept on.

I wasn't thinking nothing about them angels. I was thinking about Mama. How I want her to give me some credit about how I take care of my baby. To have her say, Imani sure do look pretty today. You sure combed her hair real neat. Got it all greased up and shining. You sure keep her clothes clean. You sure keep her smelling clean and fresh like a baby should be. You sure is a good mother.

I can't stand it when Mama pick pick pick. Sometimes I feel like I'm some kind of scab she trying to peel away. I kept right on singing to Imani. There was hundreds of them little white angels dangling off kite strings and falling down into bed before she fell to sleep.

On the third day Imani was better. I don't think she was feeling good enough to go out to school with me. But I took her on anyway. I ain't even need to be missing no more time in class. Not with all the time I missed running from *him*. It ain't like I be seeing him all the time in the cafeteria anyway. He hardly been coming to school. I don't know where he be at. But I'm hoping he stay wherever it is.

At least Imani could sleep all day in the nursery. I'm the one had to stay awake and go to my classes. Our school crazy, now that it's cold. Some rooms don't be having no heat in them. It's like you going to school at the North Pole. You got to be wearing a coat and still be sitting there freezing, with your feet so cold they go to sleep and forget they part of your body. Then there's other rooms where it's hot like a desert. Sometimes the windows swole shut and you can't get them open for a breath of cool air. Your mouth be all dry, like it got sand in it, and you be real sleepy.

My English class one of them ones out in the desert. Mr. Toliver the teacher. He a black man who wear a suit all the time, but don't never sweat in all that heat. He be real cool. I like him because he wear cologne that smell like burning wood. But Mr. Toliver take everything so serious. He be making us talk proper English in his class and keep on correcting us when we don't. We have to talk that way, he say, so we'll have a good future. Maybe he right. All I know is my head be hurting in his class when I concentrate on talking like that. It don't come natural to me, and it seem like I'm just putting on. Like I'm trying to be white.

Mr. Toliver act like his class the most important thing in the world, and if he see we ain't paying attention, he stop and lecture us. Ladies and gentlemen, he say in a voice all calm, even though you can tell he ain't calm. He say, I can stop teaching right this moment and sit down the rest of the period. I don't know how many times I have to tell you, I have mine. My car. My house. My degree. And need I remind you, I get paid if you learn or not. You need to realize I'm trying to prepare you for a world that cares nothing about you. If you think it does, you're sadly mistaken. Now let's get back to work.

On the day I come back to school, Mr. Toliver seemed like he was out in the desert with the rest of us, though. Tired and thirsty. His voice was all scratchy. When he seen we wasn't paying attention, he didn't even lecture. Halfway through the period he give up and told us to read silent at our desks. That's when I went up to him to ask for the work I had missed while I was out with Imani.

He told me to step into the hall, and he ask, What do you want it for, Tasha?

So I can catch up, I say.

Mr. Toliver ask, Oh, is that so? You don't seem to take this class very seriously. This is the second time this term you've missed days at a time, and now you waltz back into my room like some belle of the ball and expect me to catch you up.

Static. He was giving off so much, I wanted to tune him out. But I say, It ain't even like that, Mr. Toliver.

He say, *Isn't* it?

My baby been sick, I say.

Your baby *has* been sick, he say.

I flipped the switch to the way he want me to talk. Real slow and careful, I say, My baby *has* been sick, Mr. Toliver. She has had a fever and I had to stay home with her.

Well, well, well, he say. So, Miss Dawson, in your absence you haven't forgotten how to speak the English language.

Aw, stop playing with me, Mr. Toliver.

He say, I'm not playing with you. Do you think having a sick baby is an excuse?

I'm not giving you a excuse, I say to him.

An excuse, he say.

It's not an excuse, I say. I'm trying to make up what I've missed.

Let me tell you something, Tasha, he say. You have to do better than you've been doing, because the world cares nothing about you or your baby. I'll give you your assignments. Have them in by tomorrow, he say, and pointed for me to go back to class while he went on down the hall to get some water.

That night I did just what Mr. Toliver told me. By the time I finished up the work for his class and my other classes, it was something after three. Imani was sleeping real hard. I was working in bed, and she laid right next to me the whole while, not even moving.

The next morning when I got up to get Imani ready for school, she was scratching herself. I ain't see no rash on her. Just a few bumps around her neck. Mama seen Imani scratching when I was feeding her. Mama come looking under her shirt and say, Tasha, she got the chicken pox.

I say that ain't no chicken pox.

Mama say, I know the chicken pox when I see them. You had them.

I ain't want to believe her. I told Mama I'm going to call the pediatrician. Maybe he'd let me bring her by real quick and I could make it to school by lunchtime.

Mama say, Stop being a hardhead and listen to me. The doctor won't let you bring her in with the chicken pox. Call him if you don't believe me.

I was going to call the doctor, but I knew that would make Mama mad. Anyway, I was thinking she might be right.

I had to stay home from school for the next week and a half, worrying about what Mr. Toliver was thinking of me. I called up to the school for him every day for the first week. Them secretaries nem maybe never give him my message. But I told them to tell him I done my work. He ain't never call me back. I know that each day he was driving *his* car to *his* house and looking at *his* degree on his wall, and not even stutting me. He was probably thinking I'm not serious. I ended up calling this girl I hardly even know that's in all my classes, and got her to give me the assignments I was missing. That would show Mr. Toliver I wasn't no belle trying to dance my way through life. I ain't even know how he could think that about me, with me having a baby. But I knew he was thinking it. There wasn't no telling what my other teachers was thinking, even while I was trying to keep up. While I was home with Imani, who was looking worse every day.

Them bumps was popping up everywhere on her. Even in her mouth. In her head. We wasn't going to no party at no Party Time Pizza. I rubbed Imani down with calamine lotion that Mama bring home to me when she went on one of her dates. I bit off her nails to keep her from scratching. But

Imani kept on scratching. My baby looked like a monster. She ain't do nothing but whine whine whine. Scratch and scratch and cry and squeal like a little pig.

I know I was going crazy, because I almost ask Mama to keep Imani for me so I could go on back to school. Just for a day. I almost begged her to when it was starting on the second week. I want to see Mr. Toliver to explain myself. But I couldn't get out the words to even ask Mama.

I know that's why I shook my baby the way I did. Because I was feeling like I was some kind of prisoner to her and I can't never get away. I can't even fart without Imani smelling it. She always be with me. Always. So I shook her right on that day we was supposed to be going to that birthday party. When we was supposed to be having pizza with the other girls and babies. When I looked at Imani, I got to thinking about her birthday. How when it come I'm supposed to remember what a sweet day it was when I had her, and nothing about him. About how I love her.

I grabbed Imani right out her crib and shook her the way Mrs. Poole shook the baby doll. Because she was whining and I couldn't take it no more. Not one more second. Her head flopped just like that doll.

Shut up, I say to her. I want to scream. But I ain't scream, because I ain't want Mama to hear me. I say it in a mean whisper. You make me sick! You messed up everything! Just shut up and leave me alone.

I was still shaking her when I seen her face all smeared in lotion. She was looking at me like she scared of me. Like she ain't know me. I stopped shaking her. Imani was quiet, just like I told her to be. Then she bust out crying, and I thought my heart would fall right out of me. I wanted to run out that room and take me a time-out. Mrs. Poole say if your baby giving you stress and ain't old enough for a time-out, you take a time-out.

But Imani ain't want me to go. She grabbed hold of me real tight to love her. To hold her near my heart. Even after what I done. I felt like a real dog. Like some bitch that ain't even have a right to have a baby so sweet. I was glad she was so close to me so I ain't have to look at her face. I ain't even know how to say to her how sorry I was in words, so I laid down and sung her "Ten Little Angels," over and over. I don't know if she want to hear it, but I kept on singing until she sat up and smiled at me. Forgiving me like I ain't even have no right to be forgiven for.

I ain't know nothing about how I could've hurt Imani head. Gave her a brain injury. When I finally go back to school, I wasn't thinking nothing about shaking her. I went back thinking about Mr. Toliver.

All my other teachers took what work I did and then give me even more so I could be where I was supposed to be. With my mouth all dry, I went up to Mr. Toliver after class. I ain't have no excuse in my mouth. All I had was my work in my hand. Mr. Toliver looked up at me when I handed it to him. He smiled at me. Maybe like the devil would smile at you. All teeth, so you think he got something good for you. I smiled back.

Then he got out a red pen and marked a big fat F on every paper. Mr. Toliver ain't say nothing. He was still grinning and had a look on his face like he want me to say something. Something in my stupid and broke-down way. Like, You wrong, Mr. Toliver. So he could say, You *are* wrong, Mr. Toliver. And I would have to concentrate until my head was

pounding to say, No, I said exactly what I meant. *You wrong,*
Mr. Toliver.

He ain't say nothing to me the rest of the week, and I ain't
say nothing to him. I just did my work and actually looked
forward to going on to Mrs. Poole class at the end of the day,
where the temperature be normal and she don't have no fake
smiles.

Mrs. Poole wasn't smiling at all, though, when she finished
up talking about shaking babies. She say, The holidays is a
time of stress for you and your child. Girls, take a time-out if
you need one. Then she told us all to have a Merry Christmas
and she give us all a article to take home about Shaken Baby
Syndrome. I folded it up and slipped it in my book without
even bothering to look at it.

When Mrs. Poole let class out, I usually be one of the first
ones busting out the door. But I stayed around packing up
my backpack. After everybody left, Mrs. Poole ask me if I
want to talk to her about something. I was shame about what
I done to Imani. Too shame to ever tell Mama. To even tell
Eboni. I mean, it was a secret only I knew. Imani probably
ain't even remember it happened. But I did, and I forgot all
about being mad with Mrs. Poole because I ain't remember
her saying nothing about shaking a baby before. I went right
up to her desk and told her how I shook Imani. I ain't never
done it again, I say. I ain't know you shouldn't do it. I wasn't
crying or nothing when I told her.

Mrs. Poole told me to sit down. I sat right in front her, and
she say, I'm glad you told me this, Tasha. You made a mistake.
A *big* mistake, and you need to know there some mistakes
you can't never set right. You was lucky, Mrs. Poole say.

I say, I ain't never hurt my baby. I never hit her. I don't cuss her and call her names. Nothing like that. I respect her.

Mrs. Poole say, I know you respect your child. I seen you with her. You take good care of her, Tasha. You a good mother.

I almost fell out my seat. Mrs. Poole say it! I'm a good mama! Her saying that felt better than if Mr. Toliver had marked all my papers a 100.

Then she say, You not perfect, Tasha. No parent perfect. I'm not. My husband not. We raised our children together, though. Most of you girls raising your children alone. How much help you get from your mother?

There I was feeling better, and she had to ruin it by trying to get in my business.

She help, I say.

Well, that's good, Mrs. Poole say. Every parent need some help, especially a single parent. You girls is under pressure raising your kids. Talk with your mama when you feeling frustrated. When you need help. Or you can talk to me if you want, Mrs. Poole say.

And I was thinking, Yeah, right! Like I'm a-come to you like you a what? A friend? My mama?

But Mrs. Poole must be some kind of mind reader ready for the psychic telephone. She say, I know I'm not the first person you'd think to turn to, Tasha. But sometimes the one you think you'd come to last is the one you can turn to first. Then she got up. You have a nice vacation now, Tasha.

And I am. I ain't been going to no parties. When I got home from talking with Mrs. Poole that day I pulled out the decorations for Christmas like I'm a good mama. I taped our black Santa up in the window with his reindeer. Plugged in our electric candles and sat them in the front windows. Put some ribbon candy out in bowls. Got our fake tree out the basement and put ornaments on it. Imani watched me the whole time like she could tell something good was coming her first Christmas out in the world. And it was, because Aunt Mavis nem came.

I don't know, maybe Imani remember when she was inside me last year at Christmas. When Aunt Mavis nem didn't come and Christmas was nothing but silent nights and silent days. We ain't even put up the tree. Mama got a little plant that come already decorated for Christmas from Woolworth. We ain't have up nam light when every house on our block was lit up. Had been that way since Thanksgiving. Even June Bug strung some lights on Miss Odetta porch. But at our house it looked like a bunch of Jehovah Witnesses or Nation of Islam people was living up in here. Like you could come to our house and buy a *Watch Tower* or a bean pie. I wasn't stutting no Christmas, because Imani was still inside me. A secret I couldn't tell.

This year Aunt Mavis nem come on Christmas Eve. Late. Imani was already sleeping. They car was loaded down with food and presents.

Mama say, Look like ya'll moving in!

Don't it! Uncle Willis say. Believe me, sister, there ain't no food left in Virginia. Mavis bought it all.

It took him and Willis Junior and little Frankie ten trips to the car to bring everything in. The last thing Uncle Willis brung in was his big box of albums and them funny little forty-fives. Him and Aunt Mavis always bring music with them.

Seem like Aunt Mavis started cooking soon as she hit the door. She pulled out every pot and pan we had. There was water in my mouth from all the things Aunt Mavis say she was going to cook. Chitlins, black-eye peas, candied yams with marshmallows on top, sweet potato pies, greens, macaroni and cheese. She was going to make a turkey and cornbread dressing and a Smithfield ham from Virginia. Aunt Mavis let us all help make the potato pies. Mama measured the lard and flour for the crusts. But she wouldn't let Mama mix it.

Mama say, I know how to do it.

Aunt Mavis say, All you know about making pie crusts is taking some Pet Ritz shells out a plastic bag. I don't want you overmixing the dough, making it tough. You can't do nothing but sole a shoe with it then.

Mama sucked her teeth. But Aunt Mavis mixed the crusts and rolled them out. The boys peeled the potatoes, and Aunt Mavis stood over them cutting out the potato eyes. Uncle Willis ate the peels like he crazy. He put butter and sugar on them. I put the potatoes through the ricer. Aunt Mavis ain't even stand over me. She let me do it like I know what I was doing.

I wanted to season the potatoes, but Aunt Mavis laughed and say, Girl, there ain't no way I'd let a child season some potato pies. We all sat around watching her add the eggs, Pet milk, cinnamon, brown sugar, white sugar. She wasn't measuring nothing. Little Frankie moved next to Aunt Mavis. She say, If you stick your finger in this bowl, I'll break it. We all laughed because I think we was all wanting a taste. But Aunt Mavis was the one to taste it first. Then she went to adding stuff again. It wasn't until after she poured all the filling in the pie crusts that we had a chance to taste. Uncle Willis was serious as cancer. He was going two licks for our every one.

While the pies was cooking, me and the boys went in the

living room and played cards. Tunk and Rummy. Frankie ain't win and say me and Junior was cheating because he younger. We wasn't. Junior even threw him a hand and let him win. But little Frankie ain't stupid. He say, I'm a-tell Daddy you letting me win! Frankie still a baby. Still suck his thumb. We let Frankie pick something to watch on TV, and he shut up. Uncle Willis come in the living room and turn the stereo on full blast. I looked through the album covers.

He had Al Green, the Stylistics, the Dells, the Spinners, Parliament Funkadelics, the Commodores, the Jackson Five, Tavares, the Staple Singers, the Ohio Players, Smokey Robinson and the Miracles, the Three Degrees, Earth Wind and Fire, Millie Jackson, Rufus, Rick James, James Brown. Sometime when them old songs come on, at first I think it's going to be a rap song. Sound like a rap song. But it ain't. It's just somebody singing. When Uncle Willis come in to put on more music, Junior say in my ear, Help, we trapped in the seventies, and we can't get out.

I was watching Mama nem in the kitchen. Sly-like. Like I wasn't watching them. Uncle Willis was drinking some beer and singing like he can sing. Mama and Aunt Mavis was standing at the sink drinking Pepsi, Aunt Mavis was picking greens and talking real fast and loud. But I couldn't hear her over the music. Then her and Mama would both laugh and throw they heads back.

That night the boys slept in my room. Frankie kept asking a bunch of questions. How Santa Claus going to find me here? Why your blanket smell like cheese? If I can't sleep, will Santa come? Me and Junior told him Santa can find you anywhere. And I told him my blanket ain't smell like no cheese! And if he ain't be quiet and go to sleep, Santa wasn't coming for him. He started whining, but Junior let him climb inside his sleeping bag, and he sucked his thumb and went to sleep.

We all got up early on Christmas, even Imani. The boys got a video game system and a pile of games. Imani got some pop beads, clothes, and a doll. Mama give me a small boombox, a new backpack I was needing, and twenty dollars. I give her a bottle of perfume from Woolworth. Not a cheap one. But one that come with powder in a nice box. Mama say she like it. She put on the perfume.

While Mama was taking her shower and the boys and Uncle Willis was playing with the video games, with Imani crawling all over them, Aunt Mavis let me grate cheese for the macaroni and cheese while she put on the greens to cook.

She say, You know, Tasha, I like being here with you.

With me? I say.

Yeah, with you, she say. You lucky you got a girl. I always wanted me a girl to share pretty things with. She stopped pushing the greens down in the pot and come right up to me and give me a hug.

I just stood there with a piece of cheese in one hand until she lets me go.

We ate a early dinner at two o'clock. Wasn't too much talking going on, because was all greasing, stuffing ourselves like regular pigs. Uncle Willis had put a whole stack of Christmas albums on the stereo. I liked the Jackson Five one when they sang "I Saw Mommy Kissing Santa Claus."

After dinner I played video games with the boys. I ain't want to. Aunt Mavis nem was all in the kitchen, and I wanted to be with them. The grown folks. Like I was grown. I put Imani to sleep while the boys kept on playing and arguing over the top of the music about who was cheating and whose turn it was. Uncle Willis come and snatched the plug out the wall.

Junior and Frankie screamed, Daddy!

Uncle Willis say, I've had enough of ya'll yammering! I'm putting this away until tomorrow, and if you don't act right then, I'm taking it back to the store.

Frankie ask, Daddy, how you going to do that? Santa the one brung it.

Junior bust out laughing, and so did I.

Uncle Willis say, Go take a walk with Tasha. The boys liked that idea, and Mama gave me a five-dollar food stamp and say we could stop up to the Arabian store and spend it if we wanted.

It was already a lot of snow on the ground and it was snowing hard. The boys liked it, because they don't get snow down where they live. They was rolling around in it. Frankie rolled right into the street, and we had to grab him because a car was coming. That cockeye boy and these other little kids was making snow angels at the end of the block. Frankie and Junior ain't never seen that before, and they fell right out in the snow and started making angels. They was flapping they arms and legs. Come on, Frankie say, licking snot off his lips. This fun, Tasha.

I thought I was too big to be making angels. I'm a mama. But I made one, the biggest one, and then went on to the store.

That Arabian store was decorated for Christmas, with all color flashing lights going in the window. There was even a little decorated fake tree on the counter, even though I don't think the Arabians that run the store really celebrate Christmas.

We got us pop and chips and pork rinds, red hot fire balls,

and some Slim Jims. We ain't spent the whole five dollars. We got change back so the boys could play the video game by the door. It's real old. But I guess they figured it was all the playing they was going to do for the rest of the day.

While they playing they game, I snuck a peek at this one Arabian guy name Omar who work there sometime. He black like me but got that real good hair and a gold tooth in the front his mouth. Omar real fine, with a thick mustache and these sleepy eyes. He look kind of young. I can't really tell. Miss Odetta say he like black coffee. No sugar, no cream. That he got babies by black girls and he married to a Arabian woman that wear a head scarf over her face and that he don't never let come out the house. I don't know if I believe Miss Odetta. I don't know no girl he got a baby by. But he do smile at me real nice sometimes when I go in the store.

Later, in the blue-and-black silent of the night, when nobody was up but me and Imani, I went with her down the basement and got out our beat-up manger scene.

Everybody black in our manger. Mary and Joseph. Even Baby Jesus. I put ten angels on the top of it when I was a little girl. They ain't really come with the manger scene. Mama got them as ornaments one year after Christmas when things is marked down. Sometime she buy Christmas stuff like that. Ribbon and wrapping paper and bows. But the thing is, when the next Christmas come, you can't always find them.

I'd asked Mama could I put the angels with the manger scene. Mama say she ain't care what I do, so I got me some glue and put them on top the roof of the manger where I thought they should be. So they could look down on Baby Jesus. Keep watch over him. Ten little angels all dressed in white all keeping watch over one baby.

Each year I take the scene out, there be one less angel. I don't know where they go. They don't never be in the bottom of the box. This year there's just one left.

The part of me that's stupid. The part of me that believed in Santa Claus. That believed my daddy was coming to get me and take me to his life is the part of me hoping that this angel don't go. And that if it do try to climb up to heaven and fall, that it will look back and see my baby. That it will look down on my baby and see how good she is and find a reason to stay.

FIVE

Mother, May I?

Today my baby blessed. I'm the one that blessed her in the tub while I was bathing her after they dropped that ball at midnight for the New Year and all them people was there in New York on the TV, happy and screaming drunk. Imani was still up with me in the living room like there was something to see. But Aunt Mavis nem had gone, and I had took down the Christmas decorations. Mama was out with her secret boyfriend. Nothing left but just me and Imani. And then I heard some fools up the block shooting off guns. Maybe they was doing it for the New Year or maybe they just shooting like they usually be. It made me scared for Mama. I was hoping right then that she was safe inside some club someplace and not out in the street where a bullet could find its way to her. Like it was her it was looking for. Me and Imani was down on the floor anyway. But I waited until I ain't hear no more bullets before I took her upstairs to bathe her.

I ran just a little water and got in the tub with Imani. She was busy playing with these plastic rings I got her for Christmas, and I know she wasn't thinking nothing about a blessing. The idea had been right inside my mind to do it. I got up on my knees and made sure I held on to her real tight. I kept a good hold of her, like I was holding on to her for life, and bent her back gentle into the warm warm water. Back and back and back. So slow and easy she wasn't even scared. Her eyes was wide open, looking at me. She was holding on to a toy. When her head was laying on the bottom of the tub and the water was hugging her face, when it was all around her body like a blanket, I let go with one hand and scooped up a little water with the other. I poured it gentle over the top of her head, and I say, Imani Dawson, I bless you in the name of the Father and the Son and Holy Ghost. I say it to her like I have the power to say it. Like I have the right to be the one that blessed her. When I know I don't, because I'm just her mama and not some preacher that know God like he real.

Ain't no other way Imani going to be blessed in a church. Mama don't believe in it. She ain't even want me to go to the christening for Eboni two twins last Sunday. Mama say, Them niggers is just looking for gifts for them babies. If you want to take the Christmas money I give to you and waste it on some gifts for them babies, you go right ahead. What the hell kind of church is giving a blessing to bastard children anyway?

I say, It's the New Light of the Covenant Church.

It ain't no real church, Miss Odetta say.

And I'm thinking, *How you know? You probably ain't never been there.* But I ain't say that. I ain't even show that on my face. Miss Odetta was sitting on our couch like it was hers. All slouched down, with her feet all up on top our glass cocktail table. Mama never let me sit like that. And I was getting mad at Miss Odetta, because I know it was me that was going to have to Windex the tabletop when she left. She was drinking some malt liquor and smoking. I can't say she a drunk or nothing. But Miss Odetta like to drink and then be coming here, talking some trash to me and Mama.

She be funny sometimes. But sometimes she be getting on my nerves. Miss Odetta say, The preacher run that church a crackhead.

Mama ask, You know him?

And she look at me all sly where I was sitting on the floor. I smiled to myself and looked back down at the table, counting the smudges Miss Odetta dirty sneakers was making.

Miss Odetta know almost any man name you bring up, and not just men from around the way or live in Buffalo. She say she know Bill Cosby, James Brown, Billy Dee, O.J., Teddy Pendergrass, Jesse Jackson, Bob McAdoo—when the Braves was still playing basketball in Buffalo, the O'Jays, Richard Pryor, and Donna Summer—when she was a man. She even say that Rick James tried to pick her up at the Golden Nugget over on Fillmore. Before he had all them braids in his head and wasn't a freak, she say. She clean rooms at a hotel downtown. So I don't know. Maybe she done met some of them men. But I don't even be believing she know the men she say she do. I know Mama don't neither, and I wonder why they friends. I half think Mama don't even like her. I know she don't trust her. Maybe that's the best kind of friend to have, though. Some bitch you can't trust behind your back. You never have to worry about her stabbing you in the back, because you ain't going to let her get that close to you.

◆

While Miss Odetta sneakers was making more work for me, she say that June Bug sell to the preacher at New Covenant. He try to say he off that crack, but he ain't. All he is a hype, Miss Odetta say.

Me and Mama, we ain't say nothing. Mama smiled and Miss Odetta ran her tongue over her teeth and blew out a mouthful of smoke up at the ceiling.

Miss Odetta say, I can tell you don't believe me. Hey, but even a broke clock right twice a day.

Mama say, Uh-huh. Now ain't that the truth. I don't care nothing about who preaching in there. Ain't nothing going on in a church got anything to do with God.

Wait a minute, Mama say. God a man. Odetta, you know him?

I bust out laughing and cut a fart at the same time. Excuse me, I say. Mama laughed too. You a pig, Tasha, she say.

Miss Odetta ain't even laugh. She lit another cigarette even though the other one was still going in the ashtray. Drunk.

Hey, now. I don't even joke about no God, Miss Odetta say. She took a drag off her cigarette and put it in the ashtray. Matter of fact, I *do* know him, she say. He know ya'll asses too.

Mama say, He don't know me.

Yes, he do, Miss Odetta say. And he know who you sneaking around with.

Mama say, I ain't sneaking around with nobody. And even if I am, he ain't nobody husband.

Miss Odetta say, Simpkin ain't nobody husband, neither. Even though he married.

Mama and Miss Odetta both laughed and Miss Odetta lit another cigarette. Drunk.

Ain't that some shit, Miss Odetta say. I'm going to hell over some man. She reached for her malt liquor and knocked the ashtray on the floor. I rushed and got up the two cigarettes that was still burning. One of them had rolled under the couch.

Damn, Odetta, What you trying to do? Burn my goddamn house down? Mama sent me to get something to clean up the ashes. When I come back to the room with the whiskbroom, a dustpan, a wet rag, and a roll of paper towel, I was hoping Miss Odetta already was gone.

But she was still sitting there, and Mama was saying to her, You ain't going to no hell, girl. Nigger hell is right here on earth. We living it right here in these streets. Shit, if God cared anything about us, we wouldn't even be living in no ghetto. Mama looked up and seen me then and say, God ain't done nothing for me. He ain't done nothing for you neither, Tasha.

I don't really know what God done for me or ain't done for me. In the woods that night. In the dark. In the trees and quiet, I don't know if he was anywhere around. I ain't feel him inside my heart. I ain't had his name on my tongue. I ain't call on him for no help. When Mama say that about him not doing nothing for me, I was thinking she could be right. Maybe she was some broke clock ticking off two truths a day about my life. On that day I was a pig and somebody God ain't even care about.

I was thinking about what Mama say about God the morning of the christening, when I got to the New Light of the Covenant Church and seen it used to be a store. Organ music was coming out of it, leaking out from under the door like water. I ain't know if I want to go into that water with

Imani. Can't neither one of us swim. We had took two buses to get to the church, and was late because we missed one of the buses and had to wait a half hour for the next one. I had Imani all stuffed in her snowsuit. It was so much snow on the ground, I couldn't take her stroller. So she was in my arms, heavy like a bag of groceries. I wanted to go right straight back home. But it was cold and I was tired. And most of all, I ain't want to find Mama mouth wide open tick tick ticking and maybe Miss Odetta's, too. I ain't even want no static from them, so I made up my mind right then to stay. I made up my mind right then too, before I opened the door of the church, to tell them a lie about how great New Light of the Covenant was. To tell them I seen God where some Arabians used to sell lottery tickets. That I found Jesus in a place that never closed.

So I go in. The church is real dark, but I can tell it's already full up with people. They shadows to me. Sitting on benches with high backs. It's like I've come into a movie after it already started and my eyes trying to get used to things. Up front the preacher is already talking into a microphone. He dressed up in a white robe, and a light is shining on him from a stand he behind. I stop and stare at him, because he don't seem real. Seem like he's glowing in all that white, not looking nothing like a crackhead. He look like a angel that might have fall out of heaven. While I'm watching him, this woman come up next to me to show me to a seat. She's all in white, too. She even have on white gloves and a white hat like nurses be wearing in old movies.

I can't hardly see nothing. The windows is all painted over. One blue. One red. Yellow. Green. A light look like the moon is in the middle of the ceiling on a chain. It's yellow and ain't hardly giving off light. Like the moon through clouds. The whole bottom black like a piece of night. As dark as it is, I can tell a mess of dead bugs is all collected in the bottom like they in a graveyard. Looking up at the light, I trip over somebody foot. That woman catch me by the elbow and take me to a seat halfway up the aisle. I don't see Eboni nem no place. But they could have been right next to me. The devil could have been right next to me and I wouldn't have know it.

The organ music I heard when I was outside come rolling soft to me under the sound of the preacher voice. Like a wave. A old woman is sitting at a organ with a table lamp on top it. She has a wide hat on that look like a plate turned upside down on her head. I can't see her face at all. Her hat make it into a shadow. Just as soft as her music roll in, it roll back out, leaving the preacher talking and the choir behind him fanning.

It's real hot. Not just dry hot like from a heater, but wet hot like from bodies. It's like ninety-nine people that's wearing wool and breathing in a corner store where didn't used to be nothing but a clerk and a few people playing numbers and buying pop. I take off my coat and get Imani out her snowsuit. I bump elbows with this boy sitting next to me. He look like he probably in high school. I don't look too hard at him. I do what I think I should be doing. Listen to the preacher.

I'm thinking he was going to be young if he was doing crack. But he ain't real young. He ain't real old neither. He somewhere in the middle, and he's steady sweating, wiping at his face with a handkerchief as white as his robe. If he on crack, he would have been all skinny. Like them addicts be when you see them out in the cold light in the morning. All dried out. They skin ashy. They lips all cracked. They eyes all flat and empty like they dead. Like somebody stuck a big old straw in them and sucked out all they life and left them walking around like monsters from a scary movie you be scared of even in the daytime. But the preacher is fat. His neck is hanging over his collar, and his face is round, shining and greasy, even though he keep wiping it. And I'm thinking Miss Odetta ain't even know what time it is. Mama neither. That make me even hotter, and I pick up a fan from a small box stuck to the back of the bench in front of me.

White Jesus is on it. My eyes used enough to the light to see he have long hair down to his shoulders, and he's floating up in the middle of the air with light all around him. He got on a white robe, and his heart outside his body, all red and open. On the bottom is an address for Paterson Brothers Funeral Home. Serving the Black Community for 75 Years. Brothers in Christ in Your Time of Need. Imani grab at the fan, and I start fanning so she can't get at it. It's hardly making a difference, because Imani all on me, making me even hotter. I give her a bottle of cold Kool-Aid I'd made real sweet with sugar. She laid back and is good while the preacher start talking about how Jesus walked on some water of a lake.

Jesus just walked right on top of it, he say, because his friends was in a ship out there. I ain't bit more believe that than there's a real man in the real moon. The preacher say it's true, and a shot of music come from the organ so loud, I jump and my baby drop her bottle. The boy next to me pick it up. I ain't look at him. Just say thank you to his hand. The woman at the organ keep playing. Her head's leaned over so far, all I can see is the top of her head. The preacher say what Jesus did was for real. The truth.

People was talking back to the preacher. I can see some of they hands. Not like real hands. But shadow hands. Raised up like you raise your hand in school. People telling him to preach it. Voices talking back from faces I can't see. Faces that's part of the dark. Hid from me under the yellow light of the moon hanging from the ceiling on a chain. They say the preacher is telling the truth on Jesus. It seem the music saying it too. Seem like it's creeping into me, the way it roll. The way it come up the aisle shaking me all inside. Shaking at my heart. But I ain't believe no Jesus walked on no water.

The preacher say, Now you ain't got to believe me. His own friends ain't believe him, and they seen him with they own eyes. They was up in that ship like a ship of fools. Screaming and hollering because they thought they was see-ing a ghost. Now ain't that something when you own friends doubt you? It's got to make you think, What kind of friends I got? But Jesus ain't say that. He ain't think that. He say, *Be of good cheer. It is I. Be not afraid.* Now there was this one man in that ship. Peter. Doubting like the rest. But he had some courage, and let me tell you this, the brother had some nerve. Because he say to Jesus, If you really Jesus, tell me to step on out there with you. Call *me* on out. If you so bad, Jesus. If you so real, Jesus. If you so powerful, Jesus, let me walk on out on the water with you. And you know Jesus was cool. All he say. All my Lord say was, *Come!*

Now, I tell you I wouldn't have wanted to have been nowhere near Peter. Because you know the brother had to be sweating. You know the brother had to be stinking. Wasn't no deodorant back then, people. And I can tell you Peter had to be funky with the sweat of doubt. You know he must have been. Stepping out in the water. Out in the dark. Out in the night with doubt in his heart. Now tell me people. If you really ain't know, would you have stepped out? Walked out to Jesus?

Yes. Yes, Lord. Say the voices. Yes, Lord, say the dark. Yes, Lord, say the music. Say the music in my heart.

Now, people, don't you lie. Would you have stepped out in the dark? In the water. In the water. In the water. In the water. Would you have stepped out on your faith? On your faith in your heart? On your faith in Jesus. On your faith. On your faith. In Jesus. In Jezzz. In Jes-us. In Jezzz. In Jes-us. In Jezzz.

Yes, Lord. Yes, Lord. Yes, Lord. Yes, Lord. Say the dark. Say the voices. Yes, Lord in my heart.

And then they hands turn into voices clapping in the dark. Clapping and clapping and clapping. Until I look down and see my baby hands turn into a voice. She clapping with them. Her bottle hanging in her mouth.

Faith! the preacher scream, and Imani sit up. Peter stepped out on faith. That's all he had. And you know what, church? Peter walked on the water, the preacher say. Walking across the front of the church, the wide sleeves of his robes flapping. Peter strode on top the water, he say. Walking back the other way. I tell you, people. It was getting good to Peter. You know how it be when something get good to you, he say, wiping his face with his handkerchief. You know how it be when you got the feeling and you don't want to come up off it. You don't want it to stop. That's how Peter was feeling. Feeling so good, he could have skipped across the water, he say. And the preacher skip across the front of the church like kids be skipping on the playground. His robe flying all up. His robe dancing up around his legs. I bust out with a laugh. The preacher keep right on skipping. I think the boy next to me looked at me. I feel a whole flash of heat hit me like I done opened a door to a oven. I fan even harder, and the preacher step back behind his stand.

Now you know that feeling ain't last, say the preacher, breathing hard. Wiping at sweat that's coming down his face like water. Just because something good to you don't mean it's going to last. And it didn't take much to shake Peter's faith. All it took was some wind, he say. The wind come up around Peter. It blew all in his face. Whipped all at his clothes, and he fell. He fell down. In the water. In the dark. In the deep. And he say, *Lord, save me.* Save me. Lord, save me. Save me. Save me. And Jesus, you know our Lord. You know Jes-us. You know Jezzz. He picked him up. He picked up Peter. Jes-us. Picked him up, and then he say, You know what's wrong with you, Peter. You have little faith! Our Lord said it. To a man. That stepped out on faith. Jes-us then asked Peter. He asked, *Why* did you doubt me? He asked, Why did *you* doubt me? He asked, Why did you doubt *me?* And what did Pet-er Pet-er Pet-er have to say? How did Peter answer Jesus? Who had just saved his life? Who had picked him up from the deep?

Nothing, say the voices calling from the dark.

Nothing, say the preacher standing in the light. Because the Lord spoke the truth. Faith. You need faith. In your life. In your heart.

When you doubt. As soon as the wind. As soon as the storms that fill this life. Blow your way. You going to fall. Like Peter. Like Pet-er. Like Peter.

You need faith. In this life. Because we're like the children of Israel. Living in wilderness. But our wilderness is in the streets.

The preacher say this and pointed at the yellow window.

We lost in a wilderness that ain't been lost in us. It's in our hearts. And done turned us into beasts. Using drugs. Selling drugs. Selling our bodies. It's turned us against each other. Turned us into idolaters, adulterers, liars, thieves, murderers. Left us scared like children in the night.

Yes, Lord. Yes, Lord.

Left us doubting just like Peter. Wondering who can we trust? And you know the answer. Just like Peter. Jes-us. Jes-us. Jes-us. No matter how far down you fall, Jesus can pick you up, he say. Then he sung them same words. No—matter— how—far—down—you—fall—Jesus—can—pick— you—up. The choir start singing too, like it was practiced that way for a show.

Everybody in the choir stands up at the same time. Somebody starts beating on a tambourine and the choir starts stepping side to side. Rocking side to side. They feet stomping out music. They hands clapping out music. Singing that song about Jesus that ain't mean nothing to me. Singing with words I ain't know. Words that mean something to them.

And in the dark, I see people standing up. One at a time. Two. Three. They popping up like they been under water for a long time and was coming up for air. Like they can't stand to be under no longer. All around me they getting up. Coming up until I can't see nothing. Until all I can see is the dark. All I can feel is the heat, and I can't hardly breathe because it seem like all the air's over my head. The only way I going to get some is to stand up. So I do.

I put Imani down next to me in the aisle. She clapping, still holding her bottle with her teeth. Slinging it back and forth across her chin. My baby bouncing the way she do when she be dancing to music on the radio. Even though this isn't no music on the radio we listening to. This music is about Jesus. Somebody Imani ain't even know nothing about. But she act like I brung her to the New Light of the Covenant Church every Sunday. Like she one of these people I can't hardly even see.

About all I can see clear up front is the heads of the choir. Rocking back and forth. The floor shaking under my feet. It's moving with a beat and I can hear that music of the organ getting louder and louder. It's all up next to my heart. Pushing past it. Into my arms. Running down my legs. It's scaring me, how it can do that. Leaving me even hotter inside so that I'm steady fanning. Trying to cool down. Trying to find some more air.

Some woman up front. Some voice starts hollering about Jesus. Over and over. Saying, Thank you, Jesus. Thank you, Jesus. Thank you, Jesus. And the choir start singing his name over and over. Jes-us. Jezzz. Jes-us.Jezzz. While the preacher ask, Don't you want to come to Jesus this morning? Don't you want to give your life to him? He gave his life for you.

I see the preacher face then real clear in the light. Glowing. While that woman steady screaming. He say, Come on up here. It's only a short walk. Step out on faith this morning. Come on out across the water.

I'm looking to see who's going to go up there to the preacher when I see my baby crawling up the aisle! Imani headed up front. Like he was talking to her. Calling to her. I take off and grab her up in my arms before she get all the way there. Imani don't like it. She start kicking to get down when I think she seen what I seen and stopped. That woman hollering up front is Miss Lovey.

She right off to the side of the preacher, standing up with

her body jerking like there's something in it. Something trying to get out. The woman dressed like a nurse is there with her, and another two women dressed the same way. Fanning her. Miss Lovey say, Thank you, Jesus. Oh, thank you, Jesus. Oh, thank you, Lord. With her hands throwed up in the air. With her face of tears turned up to the ceiling.

The preacher humming and fanning at hisself with that handkerchief real hard. So hard it come from out his hand. Now I know I ain't crazy. I guess it's the light or something. But for a second it look like a bird up in the air. Some white bird that had come right through the ceiling. Down from the trees. Out from the wilderness and floated down to the floor.

The preacher say, Won't you come this morning?

Looking right straight at me. I can feel his eyes on me, and my feet stand still while the music roll hard up against me. Holding me up. Holding me there. Touching me like I want to be touched. In a place I need to be touched. Like when I used to be kissing on Peanut. That music in my heart. In my arms. That music in my legs making me think it is all right to take a step. Even if I don't believe what it's saying. I don't think it's lying to me. Like some boy lying to me. Like *him* lying to me that night. Out in the trees. Out in that wilderness. Like Peanut lying to me about liking me thick. Like Miss Odetta lying to me about the preacher. Like Mama lying to me about God. I think that music have truth in it, and I ain't hot no more. I don't have the fan with me. But I feel a cool starting inside of me. Pouring down on me like water. Coming down on me. I stand there looking at that preacher and he say right to me, Jes-sus. Jezzz. Jesus is in the wilderness. He's in the forest. He's in the trees.

I want to step to him. To follow his voice. Miss Lovey already there by the preacher in the light, and it seem like it might be safe to go out farther. To take a giant step like when I was little and playing Mother May I at recess. Mother may I take a giant step? Mother may I take a scissor leap? Some baby steps? Mother may I come to you? But I know Mama ain't going to like that. She ain't going to want to hear nothing about God and Jesus and the wilderness and how I feel just now. I'm thinking I could walk on water. That music could carry me right on up to the preacher. Where I could fall and he would pick me up. But I know if I go up there to him, I won't be able to lie with my face right when I get home. So instead of going forward, I back right up the aisle. A baby step. A baby step. A baby step back to my seat. Back into the dark where the moonlight is hanging over me and I see in it what looked like a man.

All during the christening I was cool and shivering like I had just stepped out the tub from a bath. The choir was quiet and the music was quiet and the voices was quiet. They had all slipped into the dark, and the only voice there was the preacher's blessing Asia and Aisha. The twins was all dressed in long white dresses and they was laid back sleep. Missing everything. Eboni was holding one and Miss Lovey the other one. They daddy was supposed to be there. But he ain't even get out of jail. Eboni say he got in a fight or something stupid like that. I couldn't tell which baby was which. But the preacher knew, because he went to each one with something look like a silver pie plate. He dipped water from it and sprinkled water over they heads. Saying, I bless you Asia Joelle Carter and Aisha Noelle Carter, in the name of the Father and the Son and Holy Ghost. Them babies ain't even wake up. If that had been Imani, ain't no way she would have slept through nobody pouring water on her head. My baby would've been all awake and paying attention. Seem like that blessing was wasted on them.

I ain't even say that to Eboni, though, when it was over. I told her everything was real nice. Which it was. Her babies got to be blessed like that and have God looking out over them special. The Holy Ghost and Jesus too! And I was thinking, Who my baby got? Just me? I made it up in my mind right then that I was going to bless her. Because a baby need a blessing. There ain't nothing in them books Mrs. Poole be making us read about a blessing. It ain't nothing Mama never talked to me about. But I left the New Light of the Covenant Church knowing I was going to bless Imani, because when I took her out that door, we was heading out into the wilderness.

Mama was sitting right on the couch when I got home. Miss Odetta, too. Drinking and smoking and her feet up making work for me before I even walked in the door. Ain't neither one of them open they mouths about the church. But the question was all on they face. Making they mouths curl up on the ends with smiles because they knew they was right. Imani was sleep by then. All wore out with the cold and wind.

I sat right down next to Mama and I say, just as big and bold as day, That church wasn't about nothing. I say it with a flat face. My baby's eyes popped right open and she stared right straight at me like she know I was lying. Miss Odetta actually sat up straight like her back wasn't broke.

Mama say, I could have told you that. Money. That's all church is about.

Miss Odetta ask, How the preacher look? Bad? Imani was still looking at me like she was understanding, so I shook my head and say I had to go put Imani down so she could get a good nap in. I was thinking of blessing her then. But I wanted to wait until we was all alone, like we was tonight.

After I blessed her, Imani got the shivers before I could get her out the tub. I ain't even let the water out. I just got her out and dried her real good and dressed her before I even dried and dressed myself. Then I put her down in her crib with a bottle and went to let the water out the tub. Before the last of it went down the drain, I was thinking that I didn't know if the blessing took. I hoped it did. That she got more than me. And then I took a few drops of water up in my hands and blessed myself.

SIX

L.O.V.E.

A LITTLE AFTER I went back to school from my Christmas break, Mama opened up her closet and pulled out a big old skeleton. Me and her and Imani was just sitting in the living room on a regular kind of Sunday. I was combing Imani head, while Mama was watching some old movie on TV. Then there was a knock at the door and Mama go to answer.

I thought it must be Miss Odetta coming over to make some work for me. But it wasn't even her. It was them bones still all up inside a white man. Mama pulled him into our living room and kissed him dead in the mouth on the rug I'd just vacuumed the day before. He the boyfriend she been keeping secret. She say his name Mitch.

It was like some bird flew inside me. Plucked out every word and flew off with them to put them in a nest. Somewhere out there in the wilderness up in some tree was my voice screaming in the wind. Mama done went and got herself a white man! When all I could do was sit there while that white man spoke to me.

He say, It's good meeting you, Tasha. Your mama has said such nice things about you.

I was thinking, *You might be telling the truth, but she ain't said nam word to me about you.*

My mouth was hanging open. All empty and dry. Mama was standing right next to him, throwing me dirty I'd-better-be-polite-now-or-she-going-to-slap-me-into-the-middle-of-next-week-later looks. I got a smile to come up out me from somewhere. A real smile. Not a fake one to stop Mama from knocking me through time when Mitch was gone and there wasn't going to be no good reason for her to be polite. It seemed to calm Mama down. I ain't mean no harm to Mitch. But no white person, let alone some white man Mama was saying was her boyfriend, ever set a foot in our house for nothing. And now here he was. And he was here for something. My mama.

Imani crawled right over to him. I don't think she cared nothing about him. All she wanted was to get away from me and the comb. Her hair was all napped up, because I hadn't done it in a week, and she was dodging the plastic comb like it was a straightening comb licking tongues of fire at her head. I was trying my best not to hurt her. I'd wet her hair and greased it good. But it was still hard to comb, and she was steady whining.

Mitch bent down like my baby was really interested in him, and say, Hello, darling.

And my baby had the nerve to reach her arms right out to him like he wasn't no stranger and white. Mitch picked her up and went and sat on the couch with Mama.

Mama say, Get me and Mitch something to drink.

Mitch say, I'll take a beer, if you got one.

Mama say, We ain't got no beer.

I say, I think Miss Odetta left one in the fridge.

Mama cut her eyes at me and say, We ain't got no beer. And even if we did, your ass ain't having nam up in here. You on your way to work, Mitch, and you know how you be when you drink.

Mitch say, It's only one little old beer, sugar.

Mama say, Bring us some Pepsi and some ice.

I went and got the drinks. Right on the shelf with the Pepsi was a beer. I picked it up but then put it back on the shelf. Shoot. If that white man was stupid enough to have Mama talk to him like he was a child with no sense, telling him what he could and couldn't have, then he was getting a Pepsi like Mama say.

When I come back in the living room, I heard Mitch say to Mama, She's so cute. If we go out with her, people will probably think she's our baby.

Mama rolled her eyes at him. Mama say, Shit, they can think what they want to think. But I got me one baby and I ain't never having no more.

I was thinking there was no way nobody was going to think my child was mixed up with nothing. Not with the nappy hair she got. I ain't like what Mitch say, anyway. Coming up into our house already claiming stuff which ain't bit more belong to him than the man in the moon.

I couldn't even look straight at him. He got this red red hair and freckles everywhere you can see and they run off into places you can't and never would want to see. I put the drinks down on the table and sat on the floor. Watching to see if he would put his shoes up on the table and start making more work for me for later. At least he kept his feet on the floor like somebody with manners. Like somebody not raised up in a barn, and he say, Thank you, darling. Didn't you get nothing for yourself?

I just shook my head.

Mitch kept pushing on trying to make a conversation where there wasn't none. So, your mama tells me you're going to be a doctor.

I looked up at Mama, and she say, She sure is. You looking at a future doctor right there.

And right there in the present, I feel like falling through the floor and all the way to China. Because all that talk about me being a doctor is turning into a big joke, because I'm failing Mr. Toliver class. Mama ain't know it right then. But report cards coming. I don't even want to see mine.

Mitch sipped on his Pepsi real polite and say to me, You listen to me, darling. Don't you let nothing keep you from your dreams. I gave up on mine too easy. I threw them away, and I'm working at the post office. And I'll tell you something. The post office is nobody's dream. It's a whole nother reality.

Mama say, Don't you even get started telling no stories up in here.

Mitch say, What story? I'm talking about my life, sugar. It's true. I wasn't much older than Tasha when I screwed my life right into the ground. Tasha, your mama has got a bad heart. She can't take hearing about nothing worrisome.

Mama say, Ain't a damn thing wrong with my heart. I just don't know why you feel you got to be telling your personal business. What make you think my child need to hear it?

For the first time I looked real direct at Mitch. Past all his freckles and into his blue eyes, and I say, I want to hear it.

Mama say, Mind your own business, girl. Ain't nobody talking to you. Mitch, go on to work before you late.

Yeah, I guess you're right, he say. He drank a big gulp of Pepsi and got up and put Imani on the floor next to me. He told me bye and walked with Mama to the door.

They stood there talking real quiet while I was wondering how Mitch screwed his life into the ground. Had somebody took a big old screwdriver to the top of his head, or had he done it hisself? I was thinking he probably done it hisself by just the way he talked. That he was probably some skinny white boy growing up out in a suburb who ain't had no better sense than to get off into drugs, never mind how many times they be telling you not to take them, and his brains got scrambled like eggs. Then he had to start stealing money from his mama pocketbook and TVs and toaster ovens from his neighbors to keep on using. Maybe he turned hisself into the kind of person his own mama ain't even trust. The kind of child you cried when you saw coming and cried when you saw leaving and in the middle time you cussed at and tried to slap sense into they heads while they just stared at the TV, because they loved you. But thought you was just they stupid mama crazy and carrying on. Maybe when Mitch gave up the drugs he was only fit to work at the post office or maybe hand out quarters at a laundromat and clean lint out of dryer filters.

What Mama wanted with him, I ain't even know. He wasn't good-looking nowhere I could see. Maybe somewhere I couldn't see, like up under the bottom of his foot, he was handsome. The next time he come over I was going to look close at his hands to see if he had one of them ink pen tattoos spelling out L.O.V.E. across the knuckles. The kind of tattoo

kids with no sense and too much time on they hands be giving each other.

Mama kissed Mitch dead in the mouth again and stuck her
hand in his back pocket where his wallet was.

Oh, I almost forgot, he say, as Mama pulled out his wallet
and handed it to him. Mitch took out some bills and put
them inside Mama bra. I don't know what was wrong with
the both of them, because they was acting like me and Imani
wasn't even there. After he put the money in Mama bra, he
squeezed her titty and whispered something that made her
laugh. She slapped his hand away and told him to quit. But I
knew she ain't want him to, because she was smiling back.

When Mitch left, Mama wiped the smile right off her face
and come back to the couch and say, So what you think of
Mitch?

Imani come back to me. I held her close like a shield and
say, I don't think nothing of him. I mean, I ain't got nothing
to say.

Mama sucked her teeth. Aw, stop lying, Tasha. You got
something to say, all right, but before you ever even *think* it.
And Mama stopped talking and pulled the money from out
her bra. This here is the money to get the cable turned back
on. Legal. It's what you want, ain't it?

I ain't say nothing. I just sat there looking at Mama.

She say, Now shut up your mouth before a bird fly in it
and build a nest.

I ain't even know my mouth was hanging open.

Maybe I should've felt grateful about what Mitch had
done. But I didn't. Mama must think I'm some stupid little
girl. She sat right down on the couch. Acting like Mitch some
kind of Santa Claus. Acting like there is really some white

man who come busting into black folks house to give they kids something for nothing. Just because they good for goodness sake. I knew there was only one way Mama could pay Mitch back for cable, and it made me turn my face away from hers, because I ain't want her to see it made me hate him.

I concentrated on doing Imani hair. Before I could even make another good, straight part, there was a knock at the door again. Mama told me to get it. I ain't want to, because I knew it had to be Miss Odetta for real.

It was. She was breathing hard like she had been running for miles, when all she did was come from right next door. It was real cold out. There was snow on the ground, but Miss Odetta ain't have on nothing but a housedress snapped up all crooked and a pair of house shoes dragging on her ashy feet. Her face was all lighted up. Not like she was drunk or nothing. But like it was full of gossip. I knew right then she knew about Mitch, and I was wondering what kind of unnatural bitch she is. Not like a bitch bitch. But like a dog. A female dog that's got some great hearing. She probably heard Mama opening up her closet door and that skeleton falling out. I was thinking right then I was going to make a stop down Woolworth basement where they keep the birds and fish and hamsters and it stink and see if they got a whistle only dogs can hear. If they got one, I'm going to get it and blow it out my window in the middle of the night to see if Miss Odetta come to our house like she did that day.

Miss Odetta was holding on to four cans of malt liquor in them plastic rings, and she pushed past me without even speaking. Like I'm nobody she even had to bother about saying a word to. One of the cans she has come loose and roll under her foot. She slipped on it and skated right by me toward the wall by the stairs, screaming, Jesus! Goddamn it!

Watch out now! I laughed even though I shouldn't have. She ain't hit the wall, anyway. She caught hold of the bannister.

Mama come up behind me and say, Damn, Odetta, is you drunk? Coming in my house falling like you trying to get a lawsuit? You know I ain't got no goddamn money.

Miss Odetta say, Girl, I ain't been drinking. She picked up her can and headed for her favorite place on the couch. She light herself a cigarette, popped open a beer and put her damn feet right up on that table. Imani had pulled herself up to the table and was standing froze right next to the ashtray with smoke all up in her face. Mrs. Poole say secondhand smoke bad for a baby lungs. She showed us this cartoon film strip about this mama and daddy smoking all day around they baby. Then it showed the same day from how it seem to the baby. Every time the parents smoked, it showed the baby puffing on its own little cigarette. But I could tell my baby was standing there because she was having a bowel movement. She had this silly look on her face like she was half-embarrassed. She ain't ready to be potty-trained, though. I picked Imani up and got her away from that smoke and took her upstairs.

By the time I got Imani all cleaned up, she was falling to sleep. I put her down on the bed and went real quiet to the top of the stairs. I know Miss Odetta. She was going to have something to say about Mitch, telling Mama all about how she know him from somewhere. Saying June Bug sold him reefer and he got a thing for black women. Saying June Bug sold him crack and he had a thing for black men.

But she wasn't talking about him. She was telling Mama about some white man she had dated.

Mama say, Get out of here, Odetta. You ain't even went out with nobody from no damn Rolling Stones.

Miss Odetta say, Yes, I did. I ain't never wanted to brag on it. To be dropping names or nothing. It was when they played out at Rich Stadium a few years ago. They was staying at the hotel, and I did too go out with one of them. I ain't saying which one it was, because he really wasn't nothing but a freak. You know how them white boys be. Wanting to do unnatural things. Stick they dick up your ass. I had to tell him, Damn, you got the right key, baby, but you working on the wrong keyhole.

Mama say, Mitch ain't nothing like that. See now, that's why I ain't even bother bringing Mitch around here until now. I know ya'll wasn't going to like him.

Miss Odetta say, I don't know who all of this ya'll is. But if you like him, I love him.

Well, you the only one loving him then, Mama say. Because you ain't going to hear me say I love him. Fuck being in love. I done been in love. And where in the hell did love get me? Mitch got money, and he spend it on me. Shit, I'm taking money from any man who's fool enough to give it to me. Spend it on me.

Miss Odetta say, Ain't nothing wrong with love. I'm in love.

Mama say, With some other woman husband? That's just some rent-to-own shit. You renting him and his wife own him. I ain't doing that again.

Miss Odetta ain't say nothing for a while. I heard her pop open another can of beer. Then she say, It's just as well you ain't in love with him. You know white men be after just one thing.

Mama ask, Is that so? What they be after, Odetta?

Miss Odetta say, You know the way white men is, especially with real real black women. They don't be thinking about love nohow. They just want to hit it and quit it. When this white man done had enough, you won't even know where he is.

Mama laughed. She say, Girl, Mitch love me. He ain't going nowhere.

Miss Odetta say, You mark my words. He ain't going to stay.

I was smoking mad, sitting on them steps with Miss Odetta talking like she ain't dark herself. She just as black as me and Mama. I could see why some white man would do it with her trifling, drinking, smoking self and keep on like a rolling stone. Much as I'd already took to hating Mitch, I wanted Miss Odetta to be wrong. I don't know why I'd been even thinking like I had. Wanting to hang on to every nasty word she say about him. Me and my crazy self should've known she'd try to wipe her nasty words on Mama too. To mark them on her.

If Mama say Mitch love her, he do. It ain't about sex and it ain't about her being black. He love her. Plain and simple because he a man and she a woman. Why can't a white man love a black woman?

I ain't stupid. I wasn't having no fantasy about Mitch taking the place of my daddy. Mama has always told me that my daddy dead, but Aunt Mavis told me when I was little that as far as she knew, he wasn't. Him and Mama never married and broke up when I was a baby. People break up. Love fail. It fade.

I ain't know nothing about that when I was a little girl, so I made up a story about my daddy. About him loving me. About him being tall and dark like trees. Big like trees, and loving me so much that when he close his eyes, he still can see me. Even though he never do see me for real and I don't know why. He loved Mama, so why can't Mitch?

I made up my mind right then to watch Mitch the next time he come over. Not to see if he got L.O.V.E. wrote on his hands, but if he got it on his face. If he have it in his mouth when he speak words to Mama. Clean and fresh.

Mitch come over the next Friday night to pick Mama up for a date. Imani was sleep and Mama was still getting ready. I let him in and told him I'd get him a drink, a beer if he want one. I wondered if he would take one behind Mama back.

He say he ain't want nothing to drink, and ask, Where's your little angel, darling?

You mean my baby? She sleep, and she ain't nobody's angel, I say.

Mitch say, Sure she is. All babies are angels in disguise.

I ask, So is all grown folks devils in disguise?

Mitch laughed. Some of them are, he say. The trouble is trying to figure out which ones.

Mitch headed for the couch and took a seat right on the edge. I sat off to the side on the floor. Watching. And not wanting him to know I was watching. So I pretended like I was watching one of them new channels we got on cable that was turned on just that morning. But I'm looking at Mitch out the corner of my eye. Holding him there. Distant. I couldn't really see him too good that way. I was close enough to get his smell, though. I don't know if it was cologne or if it was soap. But he smelled to me like summer. The way the air find its way to you before rain.

I always liked that smell from when I was little. When I would be playing out front and Mama would make me come sit on the porch before it start pouring like I was made of sugar and would melt in the rain. I always act like I ain't want to go, but whenever that smell before rain would come floating on the air, I listened for Mama to call me to her. Mama would be sitting in a lawn chair and I'd sit on the porch right by her and rest my head in her lap. Every time, she would do the same thing. Run her hand over my sweaty head while the rain fell quiet on the porch roof. She would say the same thing, too. Girl, you been out running all day, now you playing the baby. I ain't do nothing but smile, and never move. Mama never made me move.

Just the week before I went to the skating rink, before I met *him*, we'd had some hot days. Some real little girls was jumping rope on the sidewalk and singing like me and Eboni and Coco nem used to, singing about having they love for some boy spelled out in capital letters.

> Eenie Meanie Gyp-saleni,
> Oh, Ah Um-baleni, Achi Caci Liberace
> I love you.
> Capital L.O.V.E.
> Love you
> Capital L.O.V.E.
> Love you.

Like they know what they was talking about. I'd been playing kickball and dodging cars in the street with the older kids until the smell of rain come up. Mama called me and I ran to her, while them big kids kept on playing and them little girls kept on singing. I ran to Mama so she could do the same old things. Rub my head. Say I be playing the baby. And she did them things that day. For the last time.

When Mama come downstairs for her date, I took the chance to look at Mitch direct. I stared right in his face as

Mama come into the living room, wearing not nam bra and a clinging black sweater dress that was scooped out in the front. It ain't show her titties or nothing like that, though. It was real simple. Only a pretty arc of her chest showed. Smooth. Dark and shiny like the skin of chestnuts. Mitch was smiling, his face all lit up. I wished Miss Odetta could've been there right then so she could see what I did. What Mama say *is* true. Mitch love her. There was a light in Mama face, too. She smiled at Mitch. Not like she love him. But like she know she at the center of his life. Like she the sun and he the moon circling around her, doing nothing but reflecting the light that come from her.

I laid out on the couch after Mama and Mitch left, clicking through the channels over and over. Ninety-nine channels, and there wasn't really nothing on I wanted to see. Maybe because I was thinking about Mitch. I felt a little sorry for him, him trailing after Mama, being in love all by hisself.

Like I'm in love with Peanut by myself because I still don't be seeing him. He may as well be living on the other side of the world instead of two streets over. Sometimes, instead of coming right straight home from school, I go downtown because I know Peanut have to transfer to the train there. Whole bunches of kids be going after school to the mall down there, anyway. You can ride for free on your bus pass until six.

I don't always go in the mall, unless I want a slice of pizza. The people work in the stores and security guards nem act like they don't want you in there. They be looking at you like you stole something or fenna steal something. And you don't know if they looking at you like that because you a teenager or because you black, or because you black *and* a teenager.

You can feel it, though. I can feel it. What they think, how they feel. They don't open they mouths and say nothing, but you can still hear they words. Like the music they play in the stores. Soft. You can see them watching with they closed lips, saying, Get out. Get out. Get out.

I can't say how much stealing be going on. There do be fights. Almost every time I go in there, seem like some kids be fighting. Not just boys, neither. Girls be having them scratching, kicking, pulling-the-extensions-out-your-head fights. Maybe that's what scare the people who work there. What make they closed lips talk. Usually, I just go across the street to the Woolworth. I take Imani down the basement to see the animals. Then we go back upstairs. I get some doughnuts and go sit in the back of the cafeteria so I see the door. Lots of buses let kids out on the street back there. I be looking for Peanut to come through the door. Since I ain't never seen him, I called his house. I only let the phone ring once, chickened out, and hung up, because I ain't know what I was going to say if he answered.

They don't really bother reporting on the J.V. teams on the sports on TV, so I be looking for Peanut name in the sports section of the paper. Looking to see if he done made a star out of hisself. I ain't never seen his name. When South Park come and played our school, I ain't go to the game. I wanted to. All I could think was that mixed girl would be there. I ain't never seen her. But I know she probably cute and yellow with good hair and she would be there cheering for Peanut looking like that. While I would be there looking like me. I can't say I blame Peanut for wanting her. It ain't like I hate her or nothing, or even hate him. Like some fool with no light of my own in my face, I love him. I ain't some little girl who don't know what I'm talking about. I love him. With capital letters. That's why I got up and left the house that night. I picked up the phone to dial Eboni, but ended up dialing Peanut instead. I hung up real quick before his phone could ring and thought I needed to get some fresh air in my brain to wash Peanut out my mind.

I went upstairs. Without waking Imani, I stuffed her into her snowsuit, took a ten-dollar food stamp from Mama dresser drawer, and headed up to the Arabian store. Wasn't much snow on the ground, so I could use the stroller. I tied a baby blanket to the legs and handles to keep the wind out Imani face. Mrs. Poole say to do that. To keep the blanket loose so your baby can still breathe. It was already going on eleven, so I wasn't going to stay out long. Peanut mama and daddy get home from work a little after then, and I wasn't going to call they house when they home.

By the time I pushed Imani to the corner, I could see two dealers still out. I don't really be out that late, so I guess I don't know when they go in. Some of them be out when me and Imani be heading to school, and I be thinking, *Who in the world be buying crack at seven in the morning?* That night I was thinking, *Who in the world be buying crack at eleven at night?* It was real cold out, too. There wasn't no clouds to keep in the heat. Stars was showing off in the blackness while the dealers was whistling out to each other like birds from naked winter trees. One right at the corner and another up the street. They was hopping from foot to foot like they should have flew south a long time ago. They pointed at they chest as cars drove by and called to each other in codes.

When I got to the store, another dealer was standing right outside. I only started seeing him around recent. He used to go to Lincoln, but I guess he done quit. He one of the dealers that's out when I be waiting on the bus mornings. I heard somebody call him Brooklyn. I don't know if it's his real name or just the name he use when he deal. When he seen me lifting the stroller to get it up the steps to the store, he helped me lift it. I thanked Brooklyn and he come in right behind me. Omar was behind the counter. Brooklyn say to him, What up, dog? Omar say, Prices. But that's just a joke.

I grabbed one of them little plastic shopping baskets and pushed Imani to the back of the store. I got a big bag of pork rinds, a pack of cookies, and a quart of chocolate milk. I was thinking I'd better get some hot sauce for the rinds, because there was no hot sauce pack in with them and I ain't think we had none at home, when Brooklyn come right up the aisle toward me.

He ask, What's your name?

At first I ain't say nothing. Then I told him.

He say, I'm Brooklyn. You sure is looking fine tonight, Tasha. With your chocolate self.

Thank you, I say. Even though I ain't believe him, even though I know it was a line, I was wishing I had something different in my basket. Like bottled water and fruit.

Don't you go to Lincoln? he ask.

I told him I do.

He say, I quit. I ain't got time to be hanging around to get a diploma. Who them teachers think they fooling? What can you do with that piece of paper that you can't do without it?

I say, Go to college.

Brooklyn rubbed his chin like he was thinking. He say, So you one of them kind of girls?

I say, I ain't no kind of girl.

He say, Yes, you is, Tasha. Tell me, what do a brother got to do to hook up with you? He smiled. I wished he ain't smile.

Because he looked so good. His skin was dark and smooth and he had these deep dimples.

Imani woke up just then, stretching under the blanket and kicking and whining. I untied the blanket from the handles so she could see, and she got quiet. I told Brooklyn, I got to be getting my baby home. She probably want to eat. He ain't move. There wasn't a way to step around him, so I backed up and went up the far aisle. In the front, Omar was sitting on a stool watching TV. He got up and start ringing my food. Brooklyn come to the counter.

Omar, I'll get it, he say.

I was going to tell him I had my own money, but then I thought, *If he fool enough to spend it, I'll let him.* He took out the biggest roll of money I ever seen, about as big around as a Spaulding. Peeling off a fifty, he let it float onto the counter.

Omar whined, Come on, come on, I told you before. Nothing bigger than a twenty.

Brooklyn give him a twenty-dollar bill and then took a piece of paper out his pocket and wrote on it. This here my number, he say, holding it out to me. You can call me if you want to hook up. It's my beeper, he say.

I stuck the paper in my pocket. Omar went to hand him back the change.

Brooklyn say, Give it to her. You a smart girl, use it for your college fund, Tasha.

I thanked him and put it inside the bag with the food, wishing Peanut would've walked in right then. Wishing he could see Brooklyn spending money on me. *Me.*

While I was tying the blanket back on the stroller handles, Brooklyn bounced a quarter onto the counter. He say, Give me a loosie. Omar handed him a cigarette out of a open pack.

Brooklyn ask, Where my change at? Where my nickel?

Omar say, Loosies are a quarter now.

Brooklyn say, I thought you joking about them prices, Omar. I should report you for selling them. It's against the law, you know, Brooklyn say.

Omar say, You going to lecture me about the law? Buy a whole pack.

Brooklyn say, I'm trying to quit, man. He started patting his pockets. Looking for a lighter, I guess. I seen him reach deep into his front jeans pockets. And just for a second, I seen it. A gun. A big gun. Sticking in the elastic of his boxers next to his beeper. I don't think Omar seen it. If he did, he ain't act like it.

I tried not to act like it neither. My mouth had fallen open, and I closed it. Tight. Pressed my lips together. Silent. There wasn't going to be no words sitting in my mouth to be stole. Nothing Brooklyn could read on my face. No words he could hear just by looking at me. No story to be told in the wilderness by nothing or nobody.

I turned my eyes away. Turned them right where they should've been all along. To my baby. Except I ain't see her under the blanket. She had started crying, trying to kick it off. I know she wanted to see. Imani nosey. She like to see. But she might have been thinking something else.

Mrs. Poole say a baby have such a little mind. If you play peek-a-boo with them and they cover they eyes, they think the world go away. I don't know how she know a baby think like that. How anybody know. Maybe Imani was thinking the world on the other side of her blanket had went away and me with it, so I stuck both my hands under the blanket for her to hold. For her to know the world was still real. To let her know I was still there.

I wanted to get out the store, but I ain't want to leave before Brooklyn. So I stayed next to Imani, with my back to him. Pretending I was still getting her ready to go out.

Omar say, Hey, hey, come on now, no smoking.

Brooklyn say, Damn, man. You just sold me this cigarette, Omar, but you won't let a brother smoke it.

Omar say, I sold you some condoms yesterday and I won't let you use them in my store either.

Brooklyn bust out laughing. You all right, Brooklyn say to Omar. Then he say, Damn, there my ride. I got to roll, dog. He ran out the door trailing smoke behind him that floated right into my face. I waited until I seen the car pull out before I went.

Imani had started screaming by then. Her cries was little under the big open sky. I walked past the dealer who was still out there. Thinking he probably had a gun too. Walking faster when I hear him whistle, and a whistle come back. He probably had a gun too. Every day I seen dealers, in the light, I guess I knew they had guns. But I ain't think about it. I never seen the guns, so they wasn't real to me. But I seen the one Brooklyn had, with its long black handle. I was running by the time I got to the top of my street. Imani became quiet then. Maybe she knew I was scared. Knew I'd been drawn to Brooklyn, like I could swirl around the light and heat of him.

Running, I threw away the bag. Running, I let go into the wind the paper he give me. Running, I seen it catch in the air in front of me. Dancing in the night. I passed it, heading for home. Running.

June Bug come out his mama house, walking to his car, as I was putting the stroller up on the porch. He say, I ain't never seen you move so fast. Was somebody chasing you?

I was so out of breath, I could only shake my head. June

Bug looked at me a little while. Then he got in his car and drove off.

I was sleep on the couch when Mama come home, even though I'd tried to stay up. Mama come in turning off lights. I had them all on downstairs, plus the TV.

Mama say, Girl, I don't know what's wrong with you. This ain't the goddamn projects. I got to pay electric.

I say, Mama, can I ask you something?

Walking into the kitchen, walking away from me, Mama say, If you going to ask me about my date, it was fine and none of your business. Mama turned the kitchen light off.

When she come back in the living room, I say, I ain't going to ask you about that. I want to know can I sleep with you tonight?

Mama laughed. Sleep with me! Girl, you been sitting up in here watching scary movies while I was out? That's why you had all them lights on?

No, Mama, I say.

Mama nodded. She ain't believe me, because she say, Tasha, you too grown to be sleeping in the bed with me. Whatever you seen ain't nothing to be scared of. It ain't real.

She went upstairs. I went behind her. Close in the dark. In my room, I turned the light on, got into bed, and pulled the blanket over my head, shrinking the world to the space I was inside.

Maybe I am getting too grown to want to sleep with Mama. But like a baby, I still have this smallness to my mind. I don't need her hands to convince me the world I can't see from under my blanket is real. I need her hands to do more than her words. Convince me the world I see outside it — ain't.

SEVEN

Peek-a-Boo

Jesus woke me this morning way before the sun come up. Poking me all in the back. I had him under my pillow, but somehow he got loose from there in the night. The thing is, I never set out looking for Jesus, never set out wanting him. It was the last angel I went looking for last night when Mama was out with Mitch. I went rummaging through the Christmas box down the basement. I felt like I needed the angel. Like I needed something, someone to look in the face of and see eyes with love in them. Eyes with protection. Eyes to remind me my blessing had took. That it ain't fall away like water.

Since the angel wasn't there, I decided on Jesus. I started out with him on the dresser. He could see both Imani and me real clear from there. Look right at us and have no doubt about who he should be watching, but then I thought I better hide him. If Mama seen Jesus on my dresser instead of where he belonged, she'd ask what he was doing up there. I know Mama. She can take Jesus for a week at Christmas staring out his manger, but then she want him back where he belong, in the dark in the basement in a box. I took a long look at Jesus before I put him under the pillow, set his eyes in my memory so I could see them still staring at me after I put him under the pillow. I felt better knowing he was there after I had seen that body.

Day before yesterday there was a body laying on the sidewalk in front of the store by Lincoln. It wasn't covered up or nothing. I ain't know it was there at first. I was rushing with Imani because I was running late. From down the street, I could hear first bell ringing, which meant it was five minutes until second bell. I still had to drop Imani at the nursery on the first floor, go to my homeroom on the third so I wouldn't be marked absent, and then get down to the basement for Latin so I wouldn't be marked tardy. One more tardy and I'll get detention. Imani too. So I ain't pay much attention to the two police cars and this cop at the corner acting like he was directing traffic. Except he was directing kids.

Keep moving, he say. That's your bell. You're late, keep moving. Kids usually be on both sides of the street, but everybody was on this one side, so I looked to the other side and seen the body laying right out in front of Abdul's. I slowed down. And I looked. Not because I wanted to see, but because my eyes wanted to know there wasn't some trick being played on them. That they wasn't looking in on some nightmare instead of out on the world.

Seeing all the blood in front of Abdul's made everything real to my eyes. More than the body. The body could still be a person, still be a boy who fell. A boy playing a trick. But all that blood making the sidewalk in front of Abdul's red red made me turn my eyes away and look down at Imani, wishing I'd put the blanket over her face that morning. It wasn't real cold and the wind wasn't blowing, so I hadn't. She ain't act like she seen nothing. She seen me looking down at her and looked back at me, smiling like it was just another day.

There wasn't no need for me to worry about being late. Mr. Diaz had the whole school come to the auditorium for the beginning of first period.

It was all loud in the auditorium like some party was going on. Mostly every seat was filled when I come in, except them in the front. Don't nobody like to sit in the front, but I had to go down there. Coco seen me and waved for me to sit next to her in the very first row. She done got her hair braided and have all these clear beads strung on the braids. She asked me how I think it looked. I told her it looked nice.

Coco say, You know what Kente say? He say my head look like some kind of damn chandelier.

I sucked my teeth. You know he ain't got no sense, never did have none, but you love him.

And you love Peanut, she say. With his big head.

I say, For your information, I do not.

A quiet rolled down toward us as Mr. Diaz come in from the very back. He was his usual cool self when he spoke. He say the shooting had happened long before school that morning. The police say it might have even happened in the middle of the night, and the victim was a young black man. That's all he knew. He say he know some of us was upset because we might have seen the crime scene. If we want to talk to counselors, he'd call in some extra ones. We was to go to our first-period class and then we could get a pass to talk to a counselor if we needed to. Only if we was upset, not to just get out of class.

As we was leaving, Coco say, Girl, I'm going to see one of them counselors. I been traumatized.

You ain't even traumatized, I say.

Coco laughed like she was nervous. For real I am, she say. She told me she had been there when the police ask the principal if he could identify the body, but Mr. Diaz couldn't, because the boy had been shot too many times in the head. Mr. Diaz just made the sign of the cross over the body and prayed. Coco say she ain't think he supposed to do that. Pray. On account he a principal. But she say she guess it was all right, because he wasn't on school property. Even though Mr. Diaz ain't say it, Coco say everybody know it was a Lincoln student.

Right then I got to thinking that it might be *him*. I put it out my mind, though. Even though I ain't see him all day. When the six o'clock news come on that evening, I found out it wasn't him. It was a boy named Stephan Richardson. He was nineteen. The announcer say the police thought his killing was gang-related.

Miss Odetta wasn't there, so Mama was free to say to me what she wanted to say with her mouth instead of with her eyes. That's what he get, Mama say. The little bastard was probably just getting paid back for something he did. He probably killed somebody hisself.

I say, Mama, you don't know that.

Mama say, Don't tell me what I don't know. What them boys don't know is they doing the work of the white man.

I was sitting far away from Mama, so I ask, They working for Mitch?

Mama cut her eyes at me. You know what I mean, she say. Just don't you never bring one of them little thugs up in this house.

I say, Come on, Mama. I don't even like boys like that.

Eboni called me later to tell me Stephan lived one building

over from her in Fairfield. Everybody called him Sweet. She say she ain't really know Sweet, but he was running with a gang. My mama went to a prayer vigil his mama nem had for him, Eboni say. Out in front his building. They was going to have it at Abdul's, but he ain't want them there, driving away business.

I was up in my room with Imani, supposed to be doing some homework for Mr. Toliver. I filled in answers while I talked. I told Eboni about what Mama say, about him deserving it, about him probably killing somebody.

Eboni say, Maybe he did. I just hope he asked for forgiveness in time.

I ask, In time for what?

Eboni say, For his soul to be saved. He was already saved right in our church, but he stopped coming.

I ask Eboni then if God forgive you no matter what you done.

She say, Reverend say he do. It ain't easy for God. It's as hard for him to forgive people as it is for people to forgive people. But if you ask and you be serious, God forgive you.

I shook my head like Eboni could see me. I ask, You mean if you took out a gun and killed ten people, and then say, Oh, God, I'm sorry, he going to forgive you?

Eboni say, He will, but you'd probably have to ask and keep on asking. Reverend say God a mystery.

God *is* a mystery to me. Maybe that's why Mama don't have nothing to do with him. It could be like she say — God ain't done nothing for her. But maybe Mama don't want him to. She don't like the way he do his business in mystery. She ain't got time to be trying to figure him out. What Eboni say ain't make much sense to me. How come you going to forgive somebody for anything they do?

No matter what God might do about *him*, I ain't never going to forgive him. Maybe he went to God later that night. Got down on his knees to God the way he had me on my knees. In the dark. In the night. Full up with shame. When there was nobody around to see. If he ain't have it in him to lay hisself out in front of God, maybe he prayed in his mind. Did he ask God to forgive him? And if he did. If he asked like he was serious. If he asked enough times. Like he was some child begging his mama for candy. Like he was a child begging his mama for cookies. Did God forgive him? Did God see something in him that looked like sweetness? Something that shined out of him like love?

That night after I talked to Eboni, when I was in bed with the covers over my head, I was wondering if God seen me with *him* that night. If I was somewhere in his eyes. I didn't see him nowhere in the tops of the trees. Nowhere in the dirt. I got to think God was there somewhere. Far past the stars. Did he look at me and just look away? Did he close his eyes and I just disappeared? Maybe God couldn't stop him because Imani had to come to me that way. But why couldn't she come another way? That boy could've loved me. He could've acted like he did. Said sweet words like he did when we was inside the Skate-A-Rama. Words I knew was lies. Words I wanted to hear. He could've poured them into my ears until he filled up all the empty spaces in my head and I believed them. Then I would've loved him even if God was watching. Silent.

I looked out from under my covers that night. Opened my face to the dark, hoping I would see God. Hoping I would see his eyes shining in the dark. But I ain't. And I ain't see them in the light yesterday morning when I went to school and seen the front of Abdul's. The sidewalk was cleaner than it's ever been. It ain't look like nobody died there. The only way you could tell Sweet was killed there was because somebody had put up a memorial on the side of the building.

R.I.P. STEPHAN RICHARDSON
A.K.A. "SWEET" 1977–1996
GONE BUT NOT FORGOTTEN.

Seem like memorials be everywhere now. On the sides of buildings. On phone booths. On street signs. Inside the girls' bathroom at school. R.I.P. Little Man. R.I.P. Hakeem. R.I.P. Boo Boo. R.I.P. Zave. R.I.P. Tia. R.I.P. Red. R.I.P. Greg. I open my eyes to them and then I shut them. Even with my eyes shut, I can still see the ages. I ain't never seen a memorial where the person resting in peace was older than twenty-one. I do the math real quick in my head, and it's always twenty-one or under.

I don't know who be putting up the memorials. You don't never see nobody doing them. I know it's got to be the friends of the kids who get killed. But you don't see them. Maybe some of them work way in the deepest part of the night when everybody else sleep. The part of the night so deep, even drug dealers be sleeping. Dreaming theyselves into some other world where there ain't no names on walls.

I know the kids who write the memorials put them up to make people remember even when they want to forget. To forget the names. To have amnesia. Or pretend like they do and look away. Maybe I see and don't see them memorials because I never knew none of the kids killed. I ain't know Sweet, but he seemed real to me because I seen his blood. Seen his body. Seen how quick the next day everything can be erased. How Abdul was back open for business, his sidewalk all clean, and how at the end of the schoolday even Sweet name was gone off the side of the store. His memorial painted over. White.

I felt a need in me to cry when I seen his name gone. Maybe Sweet was a dealer. Maybe he killed somebody, like Mama say. But most kids who got they name up in a memorial ain't done nothing to nobody. I know that. God must know it, I figure.

That's why I went to find my angel last night. To find somebody closer, to look right straight in the eye and have it look back at me. So I could be remembered to God. So he wouldn't forget my blessing. I don't know if he blessed them kids who was killed. If he saved any of them, or if he just watched them die. If he just peeked and then turned away with them in the back of his eyes. Fading.

EIGHT

Tell, Tell

JUNE BUG came by here today with his mind all confused. He must have been thinking it's already April and I ain't nothing but a fool. I can't believe there is some other reason for him thinking I'd go out with him. On a date. He should've been happy I even let him in the house in the first place. That I didn't just hold the curtain back and look at him and walk back over to the couch and sit down.

But it was snowing and blowing and real cold out, so I opened the door. The storm door was locked and I talked to him through it. I say, If you looking for your mama, she ain't here.

He say, I know. Let me in.

I say, Not by the hair of my chinny chin chin.

June Bug say, Dag, Tasha, stop playing. It's cold as a mug out here.

I say, My mama ain't home. What you want in here?

He say, You.

I say, Goodbye and pushed the door up while he was steady saying, Wait wait wait. Let me just leave this for my mama.

I looked to see him hold up a plastic grocery bag with the handles tied.

My mind started zip-zip-zipping. I know he wasn't even coming here trying to leave some package at our house. All I could think it was was some crack. June Bug must've shined some light inside my head while I was standing right there wide awake, because he say, Girl, You need to quit. I told you it's for my mama.

June Bug say Miss Odetta got the locks changed. He ain't have a key and ain't want to leave the package on they porch or inside they storm door. I know she got the locks changed. She got robbed almost a month ago, a little before Mama and Mitch took a trip to Toronto.

That night Miss Odetta come running to our house around midnight all loud and wild, blamming on our front door. Screaming out for Mama like she was crazy. Mama got up. I could hear her cussing all the way down the steps. I got up too because I ain't know what was going on.

Miss Odetta pushed right on in past Mama, heading for the living room. Girl, some nigger done broke in my house and turned the place upside down, Miss Odetta say.

Mama walked on in behind her and I sat down at the top of the stairs. A light come on in the living room. Mama ask, When did it happen?

Miss Odetta say, all loud, When did it happen? How the hell I know when did it happen? What I look like? A psychic? I been out with Simpkin until just a few minutes ago. I come home to see shit throwed everywhere. Did you hear anything?

Mama say she ain't.

Then Miss Odetta say, Maybe Tasha woke. She might have heard something.

I say I was up. Like I could sleep through all that loud talking.

I went down the steps. The light was brighter in the living room and it made my eyes water. Miss Odetta was all dressed up, sitting on the couch and holding tight to a big old pocketbook. Like she thought me or Mama was going to steal it. I don't know if she was drunk or what. She smelled like she had been drinking, but she ain't act drunk. Maybe getting robbed make anybody sober. I told her I ain't hear nothing. Which was the truth.

Miss Odetta say, Whoever it was come in through the back. Climbed over top of my porch and come through the bedroom window. The nigger left footprints across my white bedspread like he was walking on the floor. Your bedroom around the back, but you ain't heard shit?

Mama threw one hand up to Miss Odetta like she was directing traffic. And the sign she was throwing was one to stop. Mama say, all loud, You hold it right there, Odetta. I'm sorry you got robbed, but don't you even be thinking you coming up in my goddamn house and talking to my child any old kind of way. She ain't no goddamn watchdog.

Miss Odetta say, Girl, I'm sorry. I don't mean no harm. I'm upset. My nerves shot. I mean, goddamn, wouldn't you be upset if someone broke in here?

Mama say Miss Odetta should call the police.

Miss Odetta say she wouldn't. Right then, I know me and Mama was thinking the same thing. Mama threw me a look that I caught out the corner of my eye without letting Miss Odetta see. This all must have had something to do with June Bug. With drugs. With money. Why else she ain't want to call the police?

Miss Odetta hands was all shaking when she pulled a pack of cigarettes out her pocketbook. She kept fishing around, I guess for her lighter. But she ain't pulled out no lighter. She pulled out a gun with her hands still shaking and lay it on the table.

You'd think that all the birds of the trees be asleep at that time of night. But I must have startled a whole flock of them awake, because they flew into my mouth that was hanging wide open and taking away all the words. I was thinking that maybe it was so late that I wasn't seeing right. I was only imagining that, along with the remote control and the TV section of the newspaper, there was a gun all silver and shining laying on the cocktail table.

Miss Odetta ask me to go light her cigarette on the stove. I just stood there. Miss Odetta seen I was looking at the gun. So did Mama.

Mama say, Goddamn, Odetta put that thing back in your purse. You carrying it around like it's some toy.

Miss Odetta put it back inside and say, June Bug can get you one. Every woman should have at least a thirty-eight. If I'd been home tonight, I would have killed me some mother-fucking body. Breaking in my house!

I went quick to light the cigarette. Glad that Miss Odetta wasn't home when her house got robbed. She ain't even need to be shooting no gun at nobody. When I come back and give her the cigarette, Miss Odetta kicked off her runover shoes and put her feet up on the table. Her feet smelled all stink like some spoiled milk, and she had a hole in the toes of both stockings where the nails was all long and had scratched they way through. Probably trying to get away from the funk.

Mama let out a yawn while I headed straight for the steps. I got Imani out of her bed and put her in bed next to me. Imani was asleep, but I was still up when Miss Odetta left and Mama come into my room.

Without saying nam word, Mama put the light on and went and lifted up my window. She lowered the storm window and then let down the inside window, locking it tight.

I ask Mama, What kind of gun was that?

Mama say, I think it's a nine millimeter. Something like that.

I ask, Is that the size of the bullets? Wide? They nine millimeters?

Mama say, I look like I run a pawnshop or something? I don't know about guns. That's probably June Bug gun, anyway. Not Odetta's. She just holding it for him.

I looked at the window and ask Mama real soft, Could a bullet come through the wall? Remember that old woman was killed and one came right through the wall?

Mama say, Tasha, shut up and go to sleep.

I knew Mama was scared. Maybe she was like me, not sure what she was more afraid of. That somebody broke into Miss Odetta house. Or that somebody that drink like Miss Odetta, somebody whose hands shake like leaves in the wind, carrying a gun.

When Mama left the room, I reached under the pillow to find Jesus. He wasn't there. I looked under the covers, under the bed. Jesus was gone. I guess he went off to join the angels. I took the covers and pillows off the bed and lay them down on the floor. I got down there with Imani. Closed them blankets over us and say into the dark, with my lips moving, quiet, I say, Jesus, tell all them angels we still here.

I felt sorry for Miss Odetta when I seen her the next morning. She was heading off to work half bent over in the wind. Behind her the sneakers on the wire in front of her house was swinging. Right above where June Bug park. June Bug I think is a real dog, a real son of a bitch, for laying up in the bed and not giving his mama a ride to work in the cold.

But when June Bug was standing on the porch today, he looked pitiful hisself. He had on this five-hundred-dollar leather jacket. I know how much it cost because I done seen it at the mall. But he ain't have on no hat and no gloves. A stream of clear snot was running out his nose. That took the hardness out his face. Snot take the hardness out of any gangster face. It made June Bug look like the June Bug who was a boy when I was a girl. I ain't slam the door in his face.

He say, Come on, Tasha, just let me wait for my mama. You know she be getting home soon. I ain't got time to be running way back over here later. I got business to take care of.

I looked at my watch. It was a quarter past four. I say, You can wait until four-thirty. That's it.

He say that's all right and I unlocked the storm door. He come inside and stamped the snow off his feet. June Bug Miss Odetta child, that's for sure. Anybody with sense would've knocked the snow off on the porch.

I picked up Imani, who had crawled up behind me, and we went into the living room. June Bug come right behind us and flopped down on the couch right where Miss Odetta like to sit and put the bag at his feet. I was fenna give him a tissue for his nose, but he wiped the snot on one of his hands and tried to play it off by running his hands down the legs on his jeans. Then he put that hand he used for a tissue right on the arm of the couch. I ain't say nothing. He was raised by Miss Odetta. He was just doing the best he could.

I sat down on the other end of the couch with Imani, trying to remember where I seen the Lysol last. If it was in the bathroom or back in the kitchen. While I thought on that, I ask him, How you like the west side?

He say, How you know that's where I moved?

I say, Your mama name still Miss Odetta, ain't it?

June Bug laughed.

He know his mama and he should've knew Miss Odetta come dragging that bone over here about him moving the day after he left. She told Mama he moved in with some girl with dreadlocks. She say, Look like the girl got a head full of snakes. Like Methuselah.

Mama say, Methuselah? What you talking about? What make you think he had a head full of them dookey Rastafarian dreads? Where that at in the Bible?

Miss Odetta say, I'm not talking about him. I'm talking about the woman. The woman. Ain't that her name? she ask. She was sitting on our couch waving around a cigarette just about half ash, and I was trying to follow it with an ashtray.

I say, No, that's Medusa.

Miss Odetta say, That's her.

I say, And she could put a curse on you. If you looked at her, she turned you into stone.

Mama say, Medusa? Come on now, Tasha. I don't pretend to be no damn Bible scholar, but I think I would remember if there was some bitch running through the Bible with snakes in her head turning niggers into stone.

I told Mama she wasn't from the Bible. She was from ancient mythology.

Mama say, Oh, that's different.

Miss Odetta pointed at Mama with the hand she was holding the cigarette in. The ash fell on the table and I got it up quick.

I don't believe Medusa from no ancient mythology, Miss Odetta say. She the skank my baby living with. Got her hair all snaked up and crazy on her head. Child too damn black and ugly to have her head that nappy. She be looking evil half the damn time too! I swear I'm going to look up and she going to be done turned my baby into a stone-cold statue. Lord, I just hope they don't have no baby. It would be a little black and crispy thing like her.

Mama say, What would be wrong with them having a black child? June Bug ain't exactly light, bright, or no damn where near white hisself. Shit, if you feel that way, then he should be with a white girl.

Miss Odetta let out a loud burp that she ain't even excuse herself for. She say, I'm just saying. You the one know about them things, anyway.

Mama say, What *things?* I don't know about no goddamn things. You mean Mitch?

Miss Odetta nodded and blew smoke out her nose and mouth at the same time. I was glad I had already put Imani in bed.

Mama waved her hand. She say, You need to quit, Odetta. Acting like I'm Whoopi Goldberg and shit. Like I never met a white man I ain't like. Let me tell you something; if I'd been setting out to meet one in the first place, Mitch ain't even the kind I would've went after. I'd a gone for one of them dark Italians look like they part nigger anyway kind of white men.

Miss Odetta say, I ain't mean nothing by it. I'm just saying, is all. I just ain't ready to be no grandma. I'm too young.

Mama laughed and so did Miss Odetta. Mama say, You older than me.

I don't think that was what Miss Odetta was worrying about. I don't think she could come right out and say she miss June Bug.

Sitting on the couch, June Bug told me he lived on the real west side. Not in the Puerto Rican west side, which is just like the east side, broke-down and raggedy. He say, I live right on the lake. You can see Canada.

I say, So? Ain't nothing special about looking in on Canada and living on funky Lake Erie.

June Bug say, Girl, you ain't got a view of nothing from here. Not a damn thing.

I say, I can see plenty from here.

June Bug laughed. He say, That's what they want you to think. Not me. They don't even want no niggers where I moved. But I'm there. Right where they don't want me.

Imani was squirming to get down, so I let her. I say, I don't want to be nowhere where people don't want me.

June Bug waved his hand at me. He say, You done changed.

I told him he was the one who changed, and he say it's true. He say but he still think like he always done. Big.

Maybe Miss Odetta got him thinking big. She always seen to it that June Bug had the best of everything. The best skates, bike, sneakers, video games, headsets, haircuts, sweats, jackets. He probably had the best drawers, too. And I know where she got some of the money for it. From Mama.

Mama used to all the time sell her some of our food

stamps. I ain't like it. Mama sold them fifty cent on a dollar. I can't say Mama ain't make out. She got money in her hand, but Miss Odetta made out better. Going to the grocery store getting food half price put even more money in her hand to spend on June Bug. Mama stopped selling them when Miss Odetta found somebody to give her a better price. Thirty cents on a dollar. I ain't even want to see what woman was desperate enough for money she'd sell her stamps that cheap.

The thing is, I ain't even stop liking June Bug when some of Mama money was going right on his back. I got to say he always looked good. He would be running around with a hundred dollars' worth of clothes on. Even in the summer. He'd wear sport jerseys. Real ones. Official ones, with the tags, while we wasn't doing nothing but playing kickball and dodgeball and hide the stick and pop the whip and football in the street. June Bug always looked like he was dressed up to go somewhere.

Like this boy called Long Legs who used to live up the block. He would be all clean every Friday during the summer. That was the day his daddy come to pick him up for the weekend. To take him over to his house on the north side. Long Legs would take a shower after lunch, dress up, and sit on his porch. He used to make us all sick, because he'd come off the porch to play and make a big deal out of it. All afternoon Long Legs would say, I can't get my clothes dirty because I'm going to my dad's. I can't go bike riding because I'm waiting on my dad. Hey, don't step on my sneakers because my daddy coming to get me.

His daddy did come get him and I think we was all jealous of him for that. Lots of kids claimed to have a daddy, but his was the only one that showed up. Regular. His was the only daddy I ever seen.

Long Legs' daddy drove a pretty car. A burgundy deuce and a quarter. It was always clean clean and shining like it was brand new. We would all gather around it like it was some spaceship that had just landed. Like Long Legs' tall daddy was some kind of alien. He would reach down and touch all our heads and smile. Like he was happy to see all of us. Sometimes he'd give us each a dollar before he left with Long Legs. Then me and June Bug and the other kids would sit on the curb where the car had been and talk about Long Legs like a dog. His daddy too.

That's a old car Long Legs' daddy drive. My daddy drive a better car than that. He drive a Lincoln. That ain't really none of Long Legs' daddy nohow. My mama told me. She pinned Long Legs on him. Long Legs think he something. Wait until next week, I'm going to scuff up his sneakers before he go. I would always stick to the same line. My daddy dead, I'd say. June Bug would always say, When I grow up, I'm going to have me a better car than that. Way better, and I ain't going to live on the east side neither. I only remember saying once that I wanted to move on the north side. Even though I'd never really been there.

June Bug reminded me I had said it. He say, You ain't planning on spending the rest of your life here, is you?

I say, Don't even be cracking on the east side. You lived here up until last week.

June Bug say he never coming back to live here. Which was fine with me.

He say, What you should do is let me take you out. Show you some things. Take you some places.

I say, You asking me out for a date?

He say he was.

That's when I had to bust him and tell him I knew he had a girlfriend. I reached over and swatted him upside his head. I say, I told you Miss Odetta done told your business.

Imani seen me swat June Bug and she started laughing.

He say, Don't you be laughing at me, you crumb crusher.

I say, You leave my baby alone. Don't you be calling her names.

June Bug say, I ain't stutting your baby. She cute, though, like you.

I rolled my eyes. I mean really, he was rapping so weak.

He told me he did live with a woman and he had other women. He could get a woman whenever he wanted one. He say he could get them like that, and he snapped his fingers. Not just them female hypes that would do anything for a hit. He say they would even do it for kibbles and bits.

I say, Get out of here. They do it to you for some dog food?

He say kibbles and bits was little pieces of broke-up crack. Crumbs. He say he respected them. People think they hos. But they ain't. He say they some of the most honest women he done ever met. They all about business. You got something they want, and they willing to pay for it. He say them other women he know is hos. Even the one he living with, because all they want is your money.

June Bug say, I know she living with me because I'm living where I'm living. Because I got me a Trooper.

He say, I want to take you out because you for real, Tasha. You honest.

I nodded. I say, I see, I'm honest. Like them hos who ain't hos.

June Bug shook his head. He say, You for real, Tasha. Like that time when we kissed.

I say, I never kissed you! Lying. Lying like a dog. When I know good and well he kissed me in between our houses one night.

I was only eleven and that would've made June Bug fourteen. It was the Fourth of July, and Miss Odetta had took him up in Canada somewhere and got fireworks. Legal. All we had before they showed up was some caps we was popping with bricks, some firecrackers that was mostly duds, and some corny sparklers. June Bug had all kinds of bottle rockets, cherry bombs, and some big big firecrackers about as thick as your thumb. He had threw one of them big firecrackers between our houses. He thought it would sound louder going off there. But it ain't go off.

I raced to get it, and he came right behind me. I can't even say what we thinking. How we thought we was going to find it in the grass in the dark. We didn't. It found us. That thing boomed like a cannon. I ain't have time to scream. I grabbed hold of June Bug and he kissed me. Right on the mouth. Maybe he seen it in a movie or something. But I done been to the movies, too. So I slapped him. I say, Let me go. I just peed on myself.

When June Bug reminded me of what I'd told him, I had to laugh. I pulled a pillow up over my face and say, I never say that.

He say, Stop lying, Tasha. I liked that you say it. I can tell you, ain't no other girl ever say nothing like that to me. He ask, You that honest with Peanut?

My heart started bamming all hard. I wanted to know what he knew about me and Peanut, but I wasn't about to ask. I threw the pillow at him and say, Your time up, June Bug. It's four-thirty.

He say, All right. Cool. I say I was going to leave, and I am. You must still be some little girl if you messing with him, Tasha. Because he ain't nothing but a boy.

I stood up, trying to give him a signal. But he sat there.

I say, You don't know what Peanut is.

June Bug stood up then. He say, I do. I don't even know him and I know what he is. Me and my partners got boys like him working for us. We buy and sell little niggers like him.

I sucked my teeth. Yeah, right, I say. Peanut too smart for something like that.

June Bug picked up the bag off the floor. Laughing. He say, Who got the money, girl? And, oh, by the way. June Bug opened the bag. This ain't nothing but a prescription for my mama. Some allergy medicine. I ain't want to leave it out. The hypes, you know.

I looked at the bottle. It was sealed. I say, You could've told me what was in it in the first place.

He say, You could've asked. You know you can trust me, girl. With your life. At the door, he say, Tell your mama hello for me.

I locked both doors behind him, knowing right then I wasn't going to tell Mama he say nothing. She was off with Mitch. Mama be with him all the time now, and I don't like it. But I don't say nothing to Mama with my two lips about her and Mitch. If I do, she might slap me.

Mama sometimes say she going to slap me clear into the middle of next week, but most of the time she just be talking.

Even when she beat me the day I had Imani. I didn't go traveling through time. I stayed right there in the room with her.

The last time she slapped me was the week before she went to Toronto, and I can't say I ain't deserve it. I was running off at the mouth and showing her no respect. But Mama know she was wrong for what she had done. I found out she took Imani down to the welfare office. Miss Odetta the one slipped up and told it with her drunk self. It was late, and I wasn't hardly paying neither one of them no mind. I was down on the floor, reading to Imani, when Miss Odetta ask Mama how it had went at the welfare office. Mama shushed her. But Miss Odetta was too drunk, or she just ain't care. Maybe it was her way of making sure I knew. Miss Odetta ask, What your caseworker say? They going to keep you on because of Imani?

I was too through with Mama right then. I snatched up Imani and stomped up the steps. Mama had kept Imani two days that week. One day when it snowed bad and another when I was running late and Imani wasn't helping things because she ain't do nothing but cry from the time I got her up. Mama was all sweet to me. Had sugar all in her mouth. She say, Tasha, go on to school. Leave Imani here. She'll be all right.

So I went on to school with no diaper bag, no stroller, no baby. Just my backpack. Anybody seeing me could think I was just some ordinary girl doing nothing but keeping one eye out for the bus and one eye out for the dealers. I was thinking that Mama was trying to help me, but she was really all the time planning. All the time using my baby.

Mama come up to my room soon as Miss Odetta left, and I accused her soon as she walked in the door. I screamed at her, You make me sick. Using my baby so you can keep on getting a check. What? You done told them welfare people Imani your child?

That's when Mama slapped me. A pain shot through my teeth. She say, I don't know who the hell you think you talking to. I brung you into this world. Don't make me take you out of it.

It took all I had to make my voice regular, but I say real calm, Mama, what did you do? Mama sat down on the foot of my bed. I sat up at the head. I felt safer there, out of close reach of Mama.

She picked Imani up and say, In the first place, you should know better than to believe what Miss Odetta say. And in the second place, you ain't got to put up with them welfare people. You ain't got to look at them when they act like they don't want to give you a check. When they act like you taking money out they own pocket.

I say, Mama, you should get a job then. I ain't say it to be smart. And Mama ain't take it like I was.

She ask, Doing what?

I told her I ain't know what. I told her maybe she should go back to school. Get her G.E.D.

Mama say, Tasha, please. She was stroking Imani hair. She had combed it nice in neat cornrows. Mama looked off in the empty space between us and say, Tasha, I can't even read.

I say, You can too read, Mama.

I know Mama don't like to read. Whenever we get something like a microwave or VCR, she don't never read the instructions. Only when she screw something up. Like when Mama put tin foil in the microwave Aunt Mavis give us for Christmas a few years back. Sparks was flying around in it like a science experiment gone crazy. Mama was screaming and I was screaming and we run out the kitchen as the glass in the door shattered. Mama rambled around in the junk drawer in the kitchen after that, and I read where it say in the instructions not to put foil in it.

Mama say, Goddamn it! Wouldn't you think them motherfuckers would put something that important on the box it come in? We could've been killed.

Mama say, I can read like a little child. Like a retard.

I say, Don't say that, Mama.

Mama started talking quiet. In a voice that was so sharp and so soft, it was cutting me and loving me all at the same time. She say, I never told you why I dropped out of school. Shame. Do you know what it's like to feel shame like that? So much you can't tell nobody? Not your mama. Not your sister. Not your friend. Nobody. What was I going to tell them? I was sick and tired of feeling stupid every goddamn day of my life. Feeling like I failed. Then I had you, and I ain't feel like that no more. Finally, I had did something right.

Mama was crying by then. I started crying too. So did Imani. Like she even knew what she was crying for. We both moved to Imani at the same time. Pulling her close. Holding her between us. Keeping her between us. Where she should be. Not Mama on one side and her on the other.

I liked it being just us with no Mitch. He all the time be busting up in the middle of things. Coming in right where he don't belong. Because he don't belong at our house. On our couch sitting right next to Mama. Laying up in the bed with her. When Mitch come over and he be playing with Imani, wrestling with her on the rug like they in the WWF, getting her hair all fuzzy, I don't say nothing. I don't say nothing when she whine and want to follow after him and Mama. Go upstairs with them at night like they her mama and daddy. I let her go. Sometimes they take her. Sometimes they don't. But I'm glad when they do. When Imani go and get in bed with them. Get right in the middle of them.

When Mama told me she was going to Toronto with Mitch, I ask, Don't you want to take Imani with ya'll?

Mama just laughed. She was all excited about her trip. She say she never been in a hotel before, only a motel. I ask Mama what was the difference, and she say it was money.

She say, You ain't scared to stay in here by yourself, is you? Maybe I can get Odetta to stay with you.

I say all loud and anxious, Don't do that!

Mama cut her eyes at me, and I thought she might be suspecting something. So I quick got control of myself and say, like I was calm and mature, I'm old enough to stay by myself for two days. Anyway, Imani going to be with me.

Mama say, And she the only one I want here with you. I'll still get Odetta to stop in and check on you.

I ask, What she need to check on me for? She need to be watching her own house.

Mama cut her eyes at me again. She say, Odetta is going to check on you.

I know Mama meant what she say, but by the day she was leaving, packing a small suitcase she'd borrowed from Miss Odetta, I already had plans to be with Peanut. It wasn't like I really even invited him. He invited his own self. I just called him the day before while Mama was at the beauty shop.

I almost backed out of the call even though Coco had done told me Peanut broke up with that mixed girl. I'd put off calling him, because I thought he know some dog had brung me some bone about him. I seen in *Seventeen* that you should be casual with a boy. If he know you chasing him, he going to run. Then I seen this other article from a different month that say ain't nothing wrong with making the first move, ain't nothing wrong with flirting. Just thinking about that advice, that clashed worse than stripes and plaids, made all the nerve drain out of me.

I let the phone ring once and was hanging it up when Peanut say, Who's this?

I ain't say nothing.

He say, Come on, now. I can hear you breathing.

Hearing his voice like that, soft in my ear, made words come to me. I say, Peanut, what kind of phone manners you got? Answering a phone like that. Ain't your mama taught you nothing?

Peanut laughed. He knew it was me. So, Tasha, What's up?

I say, Nothing. I was sweating back. Funky. I ain't know what to really make conversation about, so I ask him about school.

He say he was only passing one of his classes.

I ask, What you passing?

He say, I ain't saying, but I'm aceing one. There's still a chance I can pass the year if I hit the books.

I say, Hit the books? If you was Mike Tyson, you couldn't hit them hard enough to pass.

Peanut ask, You think so?

I say, I know so. We only got one marking period left. It's obvious you ain't passing math.

Peanut say, Girl, I need to hook up with you. You the one the brain. Maybe we can study.

I told Peanut Mama was going away on the weekend.

He say, Well, we can hook up then. I'll come over and see you and Imani.

I say, Look, I want you to come see *me*.

I told Peanut about Miss Odetta keeping a watch on me. Peanut say, Don't worry about her. He say he could come to me at night out the back and over the fence. I told him I'd call him after Miss Odetta done checked in on me.

When I got off the phone with him, I found my pack of birth control pills. It was a mess where I had missed and skipped and took them out of turn, so I took two that night and another one the next day to try to get things straight again. The ones left over I flushed down the toilet.

I couldn't wait until Mama left for Toronto. Mitch was late picking her up and she was all packed and standing at the front door, peeping out the curtains, waiting for him. There was a look on her face like she was half worried that he wasn't coming.

I was half worried about that too. All I could do was think about Peanut since I'd talked to him. I was sitting on the floor of the living room playing with a puzzle with Imani when Mitch finally pulled up.

Mama ran and sat on the couch to look like she was waiting patient, casual, and wasn't even stutting him. When Mitch come in, he say he had to stop to get the car washed and oil changed. He say, We'll bring you girls back something. He picked Imani up and kissed her. I cut my eyes at him and gave him a don't-you-be-even-trying-to-kiss-me look. Mitch read it loud and clear. He patted me on the shoulder and say, Be good darlings. Mama say, You remember what I say.

Miss Odetta ain't even come check on me that night. She

called a little before nine. I had put Imani to sleep and had a bath. I called Peanut and he picked up on the first ring and he come to me all in the dark of the night. Even the house was dark, because I wanted Miss Odetta to think I had gone up to bed.

I couldn't believe how quiet Peanut was when he come flying over the fence. He was like some animal. His feet hit the ground so quiet, you wouldn't have thought he weighed no more than a cat when he done got big. Bigger than I ever thought he would be.

Some longness has pushed into his bones. He almost tall as me, and his shoulders and back have got thick with real muscles that I could feel hard and strong when I hugged him in the kitchen.

I don't know when Peanut changed. When he started looking more like a man than a boy. It seemed sudden to me, but I know it happened a minute at a time. A day at a time. A night at a time while I was in love alone. Sitting in my bedroom with my light on. Cramming Latin in my head. Fighting the battles of the Trojan War. Solving all the problems in the algebraic world.

Peanut looked so good, I got shy with him. I couldn't look right straight in his face. He ain't have his books with him, and I was glad. I led him by the hand through the kitchen and into the living room, where we did it on the couch. Not all fast like he used to but a lot slower. A lot more like Peanut knew what he was doing. I held tight to him, smelling him all fresh like soap and deodorant while he kissed me. Feeling his long lashes tickling my face. His thin little mustache tickling my neck. We breathed every sound we wanted to make deep inside each other's throats, and the house was so quiet I could hear him moving in and out of me. In and out. He stayed long enough for us to do it again and for us to have cold pizza and pop. I don't know what time it was when Peanut got up to leave. He say he ain't want to go, and I ain't want him to. But he say he'd come back the next night.

Which he did. But later than the night before. Miss Odetta had come over that afternoon to see if me and Imani needed anything. I told her we didn't, and she say she'd check on me when she come back from the store. It was almost ten, and she hadn't come back. I'd already got Imani to sleep, and Peanut had already called, wanting to know if he could come over yet. At almost ten-thirty there was a knock at the front door. For once in my life, I was happy Miss Odetta was coming to my house, but when I opened the door I seen June Bug standing on the porch, smelling like he been drinking.

He say, Mama sent me to check on you. She got a terrible headache and can't make it. Without being invited, June Bug stepped on inside. You ain't got nobody up in here? he say, walking from the living room into the kitchen.

I followed right behind him. I say, It's just me and Imani. She sleeping already.

He say, Maybe I should check on her.

I grabbed him by the arm and say, No, you don't. You ain't going upstairs. I don't want you waking my baby.

He say, You know, you sure is growing up. Looking all good. When did you get this fine, girl?

I say, June Bug, you got to go.

He say, All right. I'm out handling my business right now, but we going to get together and talk sometime. I want to talk to you.

I say, Please, you ain't got nothing to talk to me about.

June Bug car was out front of our house, and somebody was honking his horn. You going to be all right all alone? he asked.

I asked, Is your mama going to be all right all alone? June Bug laughed.

I closed the door and peeked out the curtains. The light come on in the car when June Bug opened the door. Look like he had five other guys with him. Dealers. June Bug got in and they sat there for a while. Then I heard this bass music so deep, it rattled the glass in the front door. I thought the music was coming from June Bug car. It wasn't. It come from this car I seen gliding up the street, driving real slow, with no headlights on. I watched it pass like a ghost.

People been saying that's a game these boys be playing if they want to get in a gang. They be driving around and sometimes they be at red lights waiting for you to flash them or honk at them for them to turn on they lights. If you do, they'll wait for a green light and shoot at you when they go past. Even if they just riding down the street and you flash them, they'll do it. I let the curtain fall aside and heard June Bug nem pull out fast, they tires squealing. I guess they was all late for work.

I went on and called Peanut, and I don't know why my heart was beating all fast when June Bug was here today. If June Bug really knew something, he would know I ain't no girl no more. Not because Mama say I grown, not because Imani made me grown. Peanut did.

I became a woman that last night he was over. Peanut just kept pushing in and out of me and each time he did, I breathed inside of him and he breathed inside of me and pushed harder. I let him. All the way deep until a sound rose from a place in me that Peanut could not hold inside his mouth. He tried to push it back down in my throat with his tongue. But it floated out into the quiet of the house. A low moan that hung in the air while Peanut kept on moving and I held on to him. I could see myself in his eyes. Peanut was smiling down at me, and when he finished, he whispered, You know what this mean, don't you, Tasha?

No, I say.

Peanut say, Tonight, I made you woman.

I wasn't ready for Peanut telling me that. I ask, For real?

He say, Yeah, for real. Don't you feel like a woman?

I looked away from him, not saying nothing at first. He turned my face back to his, and I seen myself again. Right in the center of his eyes. I say, I do. But don't tell nobody. Don't tell.

NINE

Red Light, Green Light

Last night at Imani birthday party when I seen her face shining in a silver circle of candlelight, I made a wish to never tell. One to keep pressed inside my two lips so it can come true. Be true. For real.

I wished *him* dead. I wished *him* dead. I wished *him* dead.

Maybe I would've never wished it, never even thought of it, if I didn't get detention on Thursday. Mr. Toliver was the one who gave me a tardy. I can't say I wasn't late for his class. I was. Half the class was late, because between periods there was a fight in the main hall. Mr. Toliver say if we ain't stop to watch it, we would've been on time. I can't say what everybody else was doing, but I ain't stop to watch nothing. Not when I been done used up my last tardy. I missed the bus last month, got to school late, and got sent to my first detention. From then on, every time I'm late, I got to stay after school for a whole period. The kids be calling detention *jug*. I don't know why.

Jug is down a long hall in the basement. The hall all narrow and lined with rows of naked pipes that make spooky sounds when water run through them. When you walk down that hall, it's like you been swallowed by some big monster and in the end you come to its stomach. The jug.

The room real cold. It ain't got no windows, and the walls made out of cement blocks. All around the wall in the back, kids done started some kind of artwork. It ain't up high where you can see it easy, but it's along the line of the chair backs. It's a kind of mosaic made out of gum.

Even with rows of lights buzzing over your head, the room still ain't all the way light. It's like the light get swallowed up on its way down to you. Don't no fresh air get in the room, and it always smell like somebody just pooted. Not one of them loud ones, but one of them S.B.D.s. Silent But Deadly farts. Ain't no talking, eating, chewing gum, listening to headsets, or sleeping. You can do your homework or read or sit and stare off into space.

So what I look like trying to go there? What I look like stopping to watch some girls scratching and punching and kicking and trying to pull each other extensions out by the root? Even if I had the time, if I had a tardy I could use up, I would've kept on going.

When there's a main fight, it be like a fire. It's so hot that sometimes other little fires jump off from it and start burning. I almost got caught in one of them accidental fights like that once.

These two boys was going at each other like crazy right outside the gym. The next thing I know, I got jerked halfway around by my extensions. I ain't have no time to think. Heat filled my head up, and I spun right around swinging. Automatic. The girl let go of my hair and caught hold to my jacket. I could see right then she wasn't even fighting me. She was trying to get away from this other girl who already had her in a choke hold and was backing her into the lockers. She let me go and started scratching that other girl hands. I got out of that heat quick and went into the lavatory to check my head. My scalp felt like it was burning, but no braids had been pulled all the way out. A handful at the top of my head was loose.

No matter what Mr. Toliver say, I was going in the complete opposite direction of that fight before his class on Thursday. The problem was all these kids come running toward it. Pouring out of class and up the hall. I swear I could feel the heat of them like some wave rushing over me. I pressed up against the lockers, trying to slide and push myself toward the steps. But the bell rung before I even get off the first floor. There wasn't no point in trying to explain nothing to Mr. Toliver. I know he ain't want to hear no excuse from me, and I ain't want to give him nam. He'd already wrote me up.

When the jug list was read over the intercom at the end of seventh period, my name was on it. Bett-Bett oohed me, and I told her to shut up, and Mrs. Poole say, Now, Tasha, ladies don't say shut up. You know better. While she was running off at the mouth, *his* name was called. I know I heard it. I wanted to scream at Mrs. Poole and tell her to shut up. Because I know I heard it. They was way past his name by the time Mrs. Poole was quiet. The bell rung without her giving us a homework assignment, and I ran out the room.

It's a good thing the hall was crowded, because I felt the craziness rising up inside me. A part of me trying to take off. To go running. To go flying down the hall. When I ain't supposed to be scared of *him* no more. I kept telling myself that as I walked to the nursery. That I wasn't scared of him. That I'd probably heard wrong anyway. Stupid Bett-Bett. Stupid Mrs. Poole. If they'd just shut up, I would know. I knew I had to quick go get Imani no matter what. If you five minutes late getting your baby at the nursery, they suspend your baby for a day. I ain't never had that happen. I never want to have to open my two lips to explain to Mama I'm going to have to miss a day of school because Imani got suspended.

Just seeing Imani there in the nursery took some of the craziness out of me. She smiled when she seen me come through the door. Her and another girl was playing with some blocks, but Imani dropped hers soon as she seen me. She got up from where she was playing and walked toward me.

It's still strange to see Imani walking. She just started last week. Me and Mama and Mitch was watching TV when she let go of the coffee table and moved away, taking these little baby steps. I started screaming. Imani fell right down and looked at me with her eyes all big.

Mama say, What the hell the matter with you, screaming like you crazy?

I say, Imani walked. Ya'll ain't see her?

Naw, Mama say.

Mitch, who be at our house now like he think he live here, ask Mama, Darling, where's your camera? We got to get a picture.

Mama say it was in her top dresser drawer, and Mitch run to get it. It had film and batteries. That was some kind of miracle all by itself. Mama usually have one or the other.

Like when I moved up from elementary school and she was snapping snapping snapping away. She took a whole roll of me, and it turned out there wasn't no film in the camera. Mama say, Now ain't this some shit! Why these stupid people make a camera work like this?

I guess Mama ain't know because me and her don't take all so many pictures of our lives. I don't know why. Even with the loaded camera, we ain't get a picture of Imani walking that evening. After Mitch got the camera, Imani wouldn't walk no more. Mitch kneeled in the corner by the television waiting to get the picture while me and Mama kept standing Imani up and trying to get her to come to us with candy and cookies and sweet words. Imani just kept plopping right back down and laughing like we was playing some game with her.

My silly baby decided to walk in our room the next morning. I was running late for school and pulling on some sweats when Imani went tipping across the floor. She did five whole steps before she fell. I ain't have the camera and definitely ain't have no time to go get it. But I ain't scream. I was real quiet, and she fell down on her own. It would've been nice to have a picture.

Aunt Mavis nem got pictures of Junior and Little Frankie from the day they was born. Whole albums with pictures of the first time they done everything. Aunt Mavis even got pictures of herself when she was carrying them. She ain't wearing nothing but a bra and some drawers. Little Frankie say he remember the picture of him being took when he was still inside his mama. He say the flash made him blink and he seen blue spots in front his eyes. He say he can remember other things from before he was born, like this one time Uncle Willis was barbecuing and there was so much smoke it got inside Aunt Mavis and he coughed inside her. You can't tell Frankie he don't remember them things. That they ain't true.

That he just telling stories about pictures he seen. Telling stories about stories he heard. Frankie don't know he just making up things in his own mind.

I don't always be paying attention in Mrs. Poole class, but I know she ain't never said nothing about babies remembering things from before they was born. She all the time be talking about brain development, so I know Imani ain't going to have no real memories, no lasting memories, for years. She ain't going to remember nothing about her first steps or the party we had for her birthday.

We did get pictures. But I wasn't sure we would, so I took her down to Woolworth the morning of her party and got her picture took. Maybe someday Imani will say she remember the party. That she liked the icing on the cake or her ponytail holders was too tight or she wished for sneakers that she never did get. She ain't never going to be able to look at a picture of her birthday and know what I wished. I'm never going to tell her. And I'm never going to tell her she seen her daddy right before her birthday.

He did have detention. I come to the room first with Imani and got a aisle seat in the very last row. And I wasn't scared. This girl bigger than me took a seat across the aisle from me. She sat down hard and say, I mean damn, Mr. Diaz know he out of control. He got babies up in the jug and shit. She blew a big purple bubble and sucked it back into her mouth. Then she took out what looked like was a whole pack of gum from her mouth and smeared it onto the wall behind her. All the while Imani was staring all up in the girl mouth like she was watching a show.

I know Imani wanted some gum. Sometimes I give her a little piece to chew on. No more than I feel like cleaning up or I feel is safe for her to swallow. Mama say she never give me gum when I was a baby. She say when you swallow it, it stay in your stomach forever, making a bigger and bigger wad. Mama say she read somewhere that when this man died, they cut him open and found he had a ball of gum in his stomach the size of a cantaloupe. She say that was what killed him. I know that ain't even true. Mostly because Mama hardly read nothing. But I still find it best that I don't give Imani too much gum.

I give Imani her bottle then. She looked at it and made a face, but I told her straight out, she wasn't getting no gum. She took the bottle and stretched herself out in her stroller. I'd turned the stroller to face me, and I pulled it closer, hoping she would take a nap before he come in.

I ain't see him at first. I smelled him. He smelled like smoke. And I wasn't scared. Even though I stopped breathing for some seconds when he sat in the row in front of me. When I could smell him strong. Smell the smoke. My stomach started hurting. Not real bad. But it felt like it was being squeezed. Not hard, but steady. I could see the side of his face the way I seen it that night. Part with light. Part with shadow. When the proctor called my name, I wasn't scared. I stuck my hand up and pulled it down quick to let her know I was there. Then she called his close after mine. She had to call it twice, because he was all bent over a book reading. Reading. That surprised me. He don't seem like somebody who'd read a thing. But there he was, reading like he was just some regular student with nothing on his mind but his book. I took out a book and laid it open on my desk like I was going to study, but I ain't read nam word.

I kept my eyes on him. I kept my eyes on Imani. It was

them I was studying. Looking at the color of they skin. The shape of they heads. The grade of they hair. The curve in they ears. The shape of they hands. Nothing matched. Not one thing about them was the same. The more I looked, the more I seen what I done always knew. Imani ain't got nothing of his. It's just me in her. All of me.

Imani watched me look from her to him. She couldn't really tell where I was looking past her. So she sat up with her nosey self and tried to turn around. I pushed her shoulders back, trying to get her lay back down. Imani ain't like that. She bit down on the nipple of the bottle and started squealing.

The proctor say, You're going to have to keep that baby quiet.

I ain't say nothing back to her, but I wanted to ask, Or what? You going make me come back tomorrow so she can scream some more? I shushed Imani, but she wouldn't be quiet. She started turning her head back and forth, slinging the bottle. Slinging it, slinging it, slinging it. All the time she was doing her pig squeal. I tried to pull the bottle out her teeth and she got louder. She wanted to have her a tantrum. I wanted to pop her. Like we was at home. Not hard. Just a slap on the hand. I don't care what Mrs. Poole or nobody say. It work and it don't hurt. I've hit myself on the hand to see what it feel like. It don't even sting like when you hit somebody playing hot hands. But I wasn't going to take no chance hitting Imani at school. Last thing I needed was that proctor to say I be abusing my baby when all I would've been trying to do was what she said. Get Imani to be quiet.

So I did what Mrs. Poole say you really supposed to do like you got sense and good nerves. Distract your baby. I rambled around in her diaper bag and found some crackers. I was fenna give her one when the bottle flew out her mouth. Imani shut up real quick. I don't think she meant to do it. My greedy baby seen them crackers and wanted them. I give her a cracker and looked to see where the bottle landed.

It had rolled into the row in front of us. I pushed Imani aside so I could get it, but before I could, he got it. He handed it to me without saying a word. I looked right in his face. Seen his eyes. His nose. His lips. All his own. And I wasn't scared. Until I seen him smile. Like he had smiled at me that night at the roller rink. But he wasn't smiling at me. He was smiling at Imani. She'd turned herself all the way around in the stroller, and I looked up to see her smiling at him. When Imani seen me, she turned back around. I shouldn't have been scared. They faces is day and night. I shouldn't have been scared, because Imani ain't turn back around to him no more. She'd seen him and smiled at him. Then she had crackers. She burped. She had her bottle. She chewed on my key chain. She played peek-a-boo with me, and by the time we left, she'd forgot all about him.

Sometimes I would like my mind to work like that. To not hold on to things. To let them slip past like water. When I got home after school, I ain't think much about him. Mama wasn't home. She'd left a food stamp on top the television, but my stomach was still hurting, and I ain't want nothing to eat. I opened Imani a can of spaghetti, and after I fed her, we went upstairs. I laid across the bed. Imani ain't want to lay down, so I let her play.

When it started getting dark, Imani come over and stood by the bed next to me. I ain't put a light on. It got darker and darker until I could hardly see her standing there. I still ain't put on the light. Imani was quiet. Like she knew her mama was crazy. Like I'd lost my mind. When I hadn't lost it.

My mind wasn't on him, neither. I was thinking about him in other parts of me. The places where there is memory in you. Underneath your tongue. The middle of your bones. The lonesome spaces deep inside. Mrs. Poole would never say there's memory there. I would never ask her, because I'd sound as crazy as Frankie. Crazier.

Imani stayed next to me. Breathing soft. Before she disappeared into the dark, she got in bed with me and stayed there until Mama and Mitch come in. Maybe she thought I was sleeping, and I guess I did go to sleep, because it was almost nine when they come home. Imani woke me up. She was calling for Mama. She climbed out of bed and went to the door. There was a knock on the other side. I knew it was Mitch. Mama don't knock.

I say, Imani right on the other side. Don't knock her down.

The door opened slow, and Imani backed up far enough so Mitch could let her out. He picked her up and I could see them both in the light of the hall. Mitch ask, What you doing in bed this early with the lights out? You all right, girly-girl?

I ain't even feel like talking to him. I knew the best way to shut Mitch up and have him go away was to just give him a answer. I told the truth. My stomach hurt, I say.

Mama poked her head in around him. She ask, You need a laxative?

I say, Mama! I ain't want her to say nothing like that in front of Mitch.

Mama say, Don't Mama me. She flipped on the light in the room, switched her thin hips in, and sat next to me. She sat on my pillow. For a second, I was still thinking Jesus was under there. I thought she going to feel him. But then I remembered he disappeared. Mama put her hand on my forehead. Her hand was cool. I ain't want her to take it away. But she did and then ask what I ate and I told her I ain't eat. She say, You must be sick.

Mitch stepped inside the door with Imani. Mama told him, Mitch, do me favor here? Go up the corner and get Tasha a Vernor's.

I say I don't want one. It got too much ginger in it. It's nasty.

Mitch asked, You want a Canada Dry?

Mama say, Tasha don't want no Canada Dry, no Schweppes, and none of that cheap-ass Fago. I don't know how they get away with calling that damn sugarwater pop. Tasha getting the Vernor's or she getting some Pepto. There's some of that in the medicine chest.

I say, I'll take a Vernor's and some salt-and-vinegar potato chips.

Mama rolled her eyes at me and told Mitch not to bring me no chips.

Mitch took Imani with him. Soon as they went out the front door, Mama folded her arms across her chest. She asked, You pregnant, Tasha? Mama ain't act like she was mad or nothing. But her voice was all tense and her lips was drawn so tight they looked like they belonged on a white woman.

I asked, You sent Mitch to the store because you wanted to ask me that?

Mama say, I ain't stupid, girl. I know you and that big-head boy you sneaking around with ain't just holding hands. Mama meant Peanut. She knew I'd been talking to him on the phone late at night. I think she knew for a long time before she say anything to me. Probably from way back when she went to Toronto, but she ain't say nothing to me until a few weeks ago. I had just got home from school, and we was in the kitchen.

Mama say all casual, Mitch say he tried to call here last night and he never got a answer. Who you was talking to so important you ain't click over?

I was smoking mad that Mitch tattled on me. The rat. I told Mama I was talking to Eboni.

Mama say, You talk to that heifer all the time and Mitch don't have no trouble calling here.

I sat down at the table and told her I been talking to Peanut. Mama picked Imani up from the floor and sat down across from me. What the hell kind of a name is Peanut? Then she told me she wanted to meet him. I asked her what for.

Mama rolled her eyes at me real slow. She asked, You think I want you running around with some boy I ain't never seen? He could do anything to you, and what would I know to say who even did it? Someone who name Peanut. Before you fix your mouth to ask me a stupid-ass question like that again, *What I want to see him for?* look in your own child face. Mama got up and handed Imani to me and left the kitchen.

I brung Peanut home the next day after school. I ain't tell Mama he was coming. Mama was watching a soap and Miss Odetta was there, too, in her housedress, with two cigarettes burning in the ashtray and three cans of malt liquor already on the table. The tops was popped on the cans and Miss Odetta was all kicked back and way relaxed, her feet up on the cocktail table. Look like some kind of fire was burning in her eyes.

I don't think Mama seen Peanut right off. I was carrying Imani, and he was behind me. Mama ask, How my baby doing? Imani reached out for Mama and I handed her over. That's when Mama seen Peanut.

So, who is this? Mama ask, like Peanut wasn't even there.

I say, This Peanut.

Miss Odetta sat up on the couch right then like she was all of a sudden refreshed.

Mama started taking Imani out her snowsuit. She say, Don't be standing all the way over there, boy. Sit your ass down.

Peanut backed his way into a chair. I think he was afraid to take his eyes off Mama. Miss Odetta wanted another can of malt liquor. I went to get it from the fridge, and when I come back in the living room, Imani was standing next to Peanut.

Miss Odetta was asking him, Who your mama and daddy? When Peanut say who they was, she shook her head. Of course she say she know them. I sat down next to Mama.

Mama ask Peanut, So what are you to Tasha?

I ain't give him a chance to answer; I say, Me and Peanut friends.

Mama ask, What's your real name, boy?

Clyde, Peanut say, but I like Peanut.

Mama say, I'm calling you Clyde. Clyde, what are you to my daughter?

Peanut shrugged his shoulders and looked at the floor. Miss Odetta popped open her can and ask, Ya'll dating?

Ain't neither one of us say nam word. Mama looked hard at me and then at Peanut and it got real quiet in the living room. Just Miss Odetta slurping and the TV going with some white couple kissing and Mama waiting like she had all the patience in the world.

After a while, Peanut looked from under his lashes and say, I like Tasha.

Mama ask me if I liked him. I just sat there, not saying a word.

Mama say, So you do like him. Mama declared right there and then that me and Peanut was both simple.

Miss Odetta agreed. Simple, Miss Odetta say. And young. I hope ya'll don't call ya'll selves being in love, because ya'll too young to know what love is all about.

Mama say, I don't care what they think they in. She told Peanut if he want to come around to see me, he going to have to act like he had sense, because I got plenty of sense, and I knew where I was going in life.

Peanut say, Tasha going to be a doctor. She told me when we was little.

Mama ask Peanut, Where you going with your life?

Peanut smiled and I hoped he wasn't going to say he was going play in the NBA. That is exactly what he said. I just slid down the couch and pulled a pillow up over my face. I couldn't believe he'd open his two lips and tell Mama that.

Miss Odetta say, Huh! That's what my son wanted to do when he was your age.

Peanut ask, What he doing now?

Miss Odetta coughed like maybe there was something caught up in her throat.

I put the pillow down to see her take a long drink. I was thinking, *Yeah. That shut you up.*

Mama say, Let's just say this. He ain't in no NBA.

I caught Peanut eye and he looked away from me. Even

though Peanut said he wanted to go NBA, his voice was all flat. It might be a dream of his, but it seemed he know it ain't going to come true.

Peanut stood up and say, I got to be getting home.

Mama say, Clyde, you can come over here and see my daughter when *I'm* home. But don't you be sitting your ass up in here every day like you live here. You ain't taking one step up them steps to Tasha bedroom. So don't you even think about it, and if I find out you been in here when *I* ain't home, it's going to be me and you.

Peanut bust out with a laugh. Nervous. And a laugh flew out of me. But I cut it short. Imani the one was laughing all loud and long. Like she knew something.

Mama ask, What's so funny?

Me and Peanut say at the same time, Nothing.

After all that, Peanut ain't even been back over here. I guess Mama scared him off. He ain't say she has. I still go to his house, though. We still do it there sometime, so I been taking my pills regular. I got the whole pack in order. That's why I told Mama that night she could take a look at them.

I ain't pregnant, I told her. I sat up and propped my back against the wall. I ask Mama, Is that all you worry about? Me getting pregnant?

Mama say, Hell, no. I'm a mama. That ain't all I worry about. It's just one of the things, she say. You a mama. You know what I mean. Other things worry you, don't they? Mama looked straight at me.

I ask, Is Mitch spending the night? Mama say he was.

I looked at her hands. How pretty they looked. Mitch pay for her to get her nails done every week. This week they was painted pearly white, each tip with a scattering of tiny silver stars. I wanted Mama to touch me again. Like she did when she come in the room. To press some coolness into me.

I was wishing it was just her home that night, not Mitch. I like to hear her breathing in the next room. I get up and go to the bathroom, and Mama will ask, Tasha, is that you? And I say that it is. I don't know who else she think it would be. When she hear me open my room door, she know it's me, but she ask. I like hearing her voice say my name in the dark. I'm too grown to go lay with her, but I like when her voice come to me in the dark of the night. The way it float to me. Like a wave. When Mitch spend the night at our house, Mama never ask if it's me when I get up.

Mama ask, When you going to get over Mitch being white?

I say, I ain't got nothing against him being white. He just ain't none of my daddy. I don't want him thinking he is.

Mama stood up. She wagged a finger in my face. She say, In the first place, Mitch ain't trying to be your daddy. Shit, if your daddy want to be your daddy, ain't nothing stopping his ass. And in the second place, Mitch ain't none of Imani daddy neither. But who going to pay for birthday cake? Who give you the money to pay for them pictures you getting made down to Woolworth? You don't like Mitch, then you shouldn't take nothing from him. Get your baby daddy to do for his own child.

That was a open door, Mama saying that. I knew any minute Mitch would be standing in that door. He'd be back with Imani, and if I told Mama, I would be all the way crazy by then. I ain't want Mitch to see me like that. Because he ain't nothing to me.

I would've told my real daddy about everything the night it happened. About *him*. If I had my real daddy, maybe it would've never happened. He would've protected me. With his love.

Back when I was in grade school, I had a project to do—my family tree. There was this sheet with a real nice tree on it. We was all supposed to color the tree and put our ancestors in the roots and present family members in the branches. I put me and Mama, Aunt Mavis, Uncle Willis, Junior, and Little Frankie in the branches in ink.

When I told Mama I wanted to put in my daddy name, she say, Put down the state of New York.

I say, For real, Mama, I don't even know his name. It ain't on my birth certificate. I'd seen my birth certificate. In the place for his name it said, Mother Refused Information. It say the same thing on Imani's.

Mama say, He dead. What you want to know his name for?

I ain't tell her I knew he ain't dead. I just say, Because he my daddy.

Mama sighed and she told me his name Xavier.

That was all I needed to know. I say, His name sound romantic, Mama. Like in a book. Was he handsome?

Mama smiled and then seem like she caught herself and stopped smiling.

I had to fill in the roots of the tree, too, but when I ask Mama for help, she say, Ain't none of they goddamn business who back in our roots. What the hell they teaching you in that school?

I say, It's our roots. We supposed to know about our family.

Mama say, Look, my mama name Rose, and she dead.

That's all your roots. She drank herself into the ground. If your nosey teacher want to know more, tell her to bring her ass here and ask me.

I half felt like writing just that across the roots, and the state of New York for my daddy in the branches, and taking it to my teacher to be smart. But that would've been a sure F and a sure-enough whipping. I wrote *Rose* down in the roots.

It made me sad to think of her as drunk and dead and Mama acting like she ain't care nothing about her when I know she did. I seen how her face got dark. How it shut off like a light. She ain't have to say it with her lips that she loved her. That she loved my daddy. That saying his name was still sweet to her. Even if she had to stop herself. Even if she had to make her face into the dark side of the moon.

I liked that my grandmama name was a flower. So I gave my great-grandmama a flower name, too. Lily. I named my granddaddy Otis Junior and his parents Daisy and Otis Senior. Then I worked on my daddy side. I thought it would look obvious if I kept on with flower names, so I made his mama Bertha Ann. His daddy Paul Junior. I ain't want to push the juniors and seniors too far neither, so I stopped.

I got me a big fat A on the assignment. I never showed it to Mama, and she never did ask to see it. But I didn't throw it out. Not after I'd made up all them people. It didn't seem right. So I hid it in my room. I tried to find it when Imani was born so I could start a new branch, so I could put her in the green baby leaves shining with light. But I never could find it.

Like I can't never find one memory of him. My daddy ain't somebody who made me. I made him. Made him up in my mind. Made him up in my heart. I keep a space for him. Not a lonesome space. Not a dark space. But one that is lit like a night in early summer.

When I seen Mama standing in front of me, talking about Imani daddy like she knew what she even talking about, with her hands on her hips, her hands to herself, I sat right where I was, with my two lips pressed shut. I knew anything I told her that night or any night about Imani daddy wasn't going to be between just me and her. She'd tell Mitch. Push him. Pull him into a place in my life I don't never want him to be. Into my daddy space. So I kept my lips closed.

I kept them closed the next evening when Mama made me ride up to Tops with Mitch to pick up the birthday cake. She was supposed to go with us, but she was doing Imani hair, putting in a bunch of twists, and Imani was sitting still. If I was doing it, she'd be all down on the floor squirming. Mama was putting a barrette and ponytail holder on each twist. Nothing but white and purple to match the dress Imani was going to wear for her picture.

I told Mama I wasn't going with Mitch. She wound a ponytail holder around a section of Imani hair and say, I ain't stopping in the middle of Imani head to go to the store with ya'll. You going to ride your ass to Tops with Mitch when he get here and pick out a cake or tomorrow there ain't going to be no party, no pictures, no nothing.

So I got in the car with Mitch later without saying poot stank to him. When he started up the car, he had that tired jazz station on. I switched it to WBLK to see what he'd do. They was playing a rap song.

Mitch say, Come on now, Tasha. Anything but that.

I cut my eyes at him, and I ain't change the station.

Mitch say, Don't you look at me like that, girly-girl.

I ain't even think he seen me, because he wasn't looking direct at me. I sat back in the seat and still ain't change the station. Mitch looked at me, but he ain't say nothing. When we was fenna turn at the corner, a dealer walked right up to the car. Mitch shook his head and we turned up Fillmore.

They vultures, I say. I wasn't really talking to him. Just talking when I should've kept my mouth shut, because of course Mitch started up a conversation.

He say, No, they're just kids. They're not much more than babies.

I say, I guess that make them angels?

Mitch say, I wouldn't exactly say that. Mitch turned the radio off. He say, If they've got any kind of wings, I'd say it would be hawk or falcon. They're hunters.

I say, Mama the one say they vultures.

Mitch say vultures is misunderstood. They don't kill. They just live off of the dead.

I say, So that's what them dealers doing? Living off the dead. That's spooky.

He say, No, Tasha, that's life.

I ask, You learn all this about life working at the post office?

He let out a long whistle. You'd be surprised what you learn about life working at the P.O. Tax deadline is next week, he say, and we're open to midnight. Pray for me, girl, he say.

We rode on up to Main Street and stayed on it for a while when Mitch say, All they need is some guidance.

By then I really ain't mind talking. I ask, Who?

He say, Who were we talking about?

I say, Oh, yeah. What make you think they ain't got no guidance? Because they black? I guess you think they ain't got no daddies neither.

Mitch say, I didn't say that! You're the one called them vultures.

I say, I can call them whatever I want to. I'm black.

Mitch say, Oh, I get it. I'm some kind of racist. That's what you think about me, Tasha? You're riding around with a racist?

I looked out the window. I say, You the one say it, not me. You the one don't want to listen to rap.

He say, Me? Your Mama doesn't like it either. As a matter of fact, she hates it! Is she some racist?

Naw, she just old, I say. And I laughed. I ain't mean to. It just come out of me. Mitch laughed too.

We was sitting at a red light. He say, Well, then, darling, I'm old too. He turned the radio back on and put it on the jazz station. Now, that's a black man playing right there. Miles Davis.

Who? I ask.

Miles Davis. You don't know Miles Davis?

I put my hand over my mouth and pretended to yawn.

Mitch turned up the music and started waving his hands in big circles. Listen to that music. It's art about pain, about love, about life, he say.

I say, Green light.

Mitch just sat there for a few seconds and a car beeped behind him.

I say, What's wrong with you? You know, it's like red light, red light, red light, green light. Then you go. You on some of that stuff or something?

He say, real quiet, Used to be.

And I knew it. I just knew he had been. I never seen a tattoo on his hands, but I looked close at his knuckles again to be sure. Nothing.

Mitch told me about how his daddy left when he was thirteen. Mitch say that was when he screwed his life into the ground. I ain't even ask him. Mitch say his daddy just left. He got three sisters and none of them knew they parents was having problems. They hid them. He say they never had one fight that he knew of. Mitch say he hated that. They was real polite. Too damn polite, he say. He say maybe if they'd broke up some dishes, or had a fight out on the porch in front all the neighbors, maybe they would've stuck together. He say he just come home from school one day and his daddy's gone. He's left a note for the family saying he just needed some time to think. About life. Mitch say that was a lie. He found out later his daddy had another woman. He'd been seeing her for a long time.

For about a year, Mitch and his sisters seen they daddy and he paid child support, but then he up and left the state. They was living in Kentucky, and he never sent another penny. Mitch ask if I could believe that. That a man would walk off and not feed his own kids. Not care if they got sat out in the street. Because, he say, they was evicted by the sheriff. He say, Everything we owned was set blowing in the wind. I was fourteen then, and things just went from bad to worse. Mitch say they got on the welfare.

He started taking drugs then and ain't get off of them until he joined the army. Mitch say when he was on them, he was trying to fill up spaces inside hisself. He say, You know, all those years growing up without my daddy, I always wanted him to come back. I wanted to knock his damn teeth down his lying throat. But after that, I was going to forgive him. Mitch say he know that was crazy talk. But it made sense to me.

At Tops, Mitch helped me pick out a cake back in the bakery, chocolate with white icing. It was decorated with a teddy bear holding a string of balloons and was dripping with pink and yellow icing roses. We got Imani name wrote on it and *Happy First Birthday*. Mitch wanted to get balloons. But I told him Mrs. Poole say they a choking hazard, along with hot dogs and hard candy. So we ain't get balloons.

On the way back home, we rode quiet most of the way. The radio was on and I ain't know if it was still Miles Davis or who it was. I was glad for the music. Whoever it was blowing on the horn is filling in the space between us. It was already getting dark and I could see Mitch face glowing a little green from the dials on the dash. I ask him, in that growing dark, You think maybe you would've been better off without ever knowing your daddy?

Mitch scratched his chin, and it sounded rough. Sandy. He say, I can't really say. All I know is, I still needed him. Some guidance. Something. Like I said about these young guys. They need it. Something real small, darling. Something simple.

I think maybe that's what I always wanted from my daddy. Something simple. Just his arms to hold me. Just his ears to listen. Just his two lips talking to me. Soft.

When Mitch stopped at a red light a few streets up from our turn for home, I glanced out the window and seen a car with no headlights on stopped on the other side of the street.

I grabbed his arm and screamed, Don't flash them!

He say, I'm way ahead of you, darling.

Red light, red light, red light, green light. Mitch sat still for a few seconds and let the car pass on by us in the dark.

At the party last night, I ain't mind Mitch being there. When I lit the candles on the cake—one for Imani age and one for her to grow on—he flipped off the light switch and stood next to Mama. Which was close enough for me. He was with us in that circle of candlelight, and I knew Imani daddy was beyond that circle. Somewhere in the dark.

I know one day when Imani get older, when thoughts don't wash through her mind. When they settle to the bottom and stay. She going to ask, Who my daddy? Where my daddy at? What's my daddy name? I don't know what I'll say to her.

Last night is when I got to thinking it'd be so much easier if I can lie to her like Mama been lying to me. To tell Imani he dead. I can have a story about *him* with a end instead of beginnings and middles in my dreams.

I can hold Imani on my lap early on a night when she ask me and ask me and ask me about her daddy. I can say, Imani, me and your daddy was young. We was just children when we had you, but we loved each other very very much. I called your daddy Honey and he called me Sugar and he called you his Little Cupcake. Now, ain't that sweet? And Imani will nod.

Then I'll say, But sweetness don't always last. Sometimes it get washed away. Sometimes it get worn away. Sometimes it just disappear in the time it take to close your eyes. Now, close your eyes. And Imani will close her eyes. I'll watch her lids flutter like she chasing dreams, and I'll say, Now, our love was the kind to disappear. Your daddy went away from us. He died. Before Imani can ask, Why? her eyes will open. Her eyes will look up at me and I'll wave my hand over them. Cool. Gentle. Like a wind. I'll close them. Leave my hands there a moment so she can look inside the dark that my hands made like the sky. Hush, now, I'll say. Don't be sad.

It happened sudden. When his eyes was closed. Not like

you now. He died in his sleep so peaceful while he was dreaming about us, and he was happy. Don't never cry about him. Because even when some sweetness is gone, you still sometimes taste it in your mouth when you sleep.

Imani will nod while my story settle down inside her. Easy. Like it's truth. Making her lids flutter faster and faster as she try to catch up with her sweet daddy in her dreams.

My story might even seem true to me. Until I sleep. Until I dream. Knowing he still out there. Past the light. And no matter what, Imani will find out there's no sweetness in my mouth for him. Just a bitter taste. Shame.

So last night when I seen Imani face shining in that circle of light, I made my wish. Pressed it inside my two lips. Because I don't want to have to even think about him being out there. I want to have a end with him. A wall between us. Death.

That why I kept on wishing to myself last night over and over while Imani blew out her candles. First one and then the other. Leaving us quiet and alone in the dark.

TEN

Star Light, Star Bright

I CAN'T sleep in the night. I lay in my bed with the window
open. Even with Mama laying next to me, it's like I be by myself. Out in the wilderness. Out in the night. Listening. Trying to hear my own voice out in the trees. It was carried away
from me by some birds and put into they nests. Talking to the
stars. Singing to my baby.

Everybody still waiting for me to have something to say.
Waiting for me to say something about what I'm feeling.
They all watch me from the corner of they eyes. They won't
hold me in the center of they eyes. Nam one of them. They
won't have me at the center. Look at me direct where I see
myself reflected back twice. Liquid. Anchored. I know it's because they afraid of me. Afraid for me. What I'm thinking.
They know there's more in me than what coming out my two
lips. And even though they want me to open up, to spill my
guts, I think they scared of what will come out from me. That
is why they look at me the way they do. Even Mama. She so
scared, she done made me her child again. Made me a little
girl who she sleep with. She been laying in the bed with me

every night for a month. She curl herself around me like I'm in her again. With my big self. With my grown self. She be in the bed with me. Waiting for me to be born back to her. Mama the one who talk. What she be talking about, I don't always know, because sometimes I ain't listening. She like to talk so the dark ain't so empty and so big and we ain't so small inside it. Curled up along its bottom. Where it touch us and cover us. Hiding us until the morning.

I don't say nothing. I just lay with my face looking out the open window. Listening for myself in the big dark outside. Listening for my voice out in the trees. Trying to reach my baby who is dead.

I couldn't even say the word at first. For a day. For a week. For a month. Not even to myself. It's one of them words that was plucked from me. Pulled out my mouth and hid away by the birds. A whole season done changed in just a few weeks while I watch out my window at night. The late and cool blue of spring nights is already gone, and there be a heat burning in the early summer nights. Nights I can see already getting darker. A minute. A minute. A minute more each night. The leaves of the greening trees in the backyard opened they tiny leaves the size of baby hands and grew into the hands of mamas. They dark and shiny sides turned to the sun before I say the word. Last night I say it with my mind in the dark dark night with Mama next to me sharing with me the secret of her hands. A secret she done kept from me so long, I don't remember her hands being so soft. Being so small and smooth. Having the power of something so gentle flowing through them that when she touch me with my face turned away from her, with my face turned out to the night. When she rub one of her hands down my arm, across my leg,

I cry. Just tears. Not even a sound, and I don't know Mama even know I be crying, and if she do know, she think it's because Imani dead. Now and forever. But that ain't why I be crying.

I be crying because it's all my fault, and if any one of them knew they'd stop loving me. I want them to stop. There's so much love for me that I can't even stand it. I don't want it. From Aunt Mavis. From Eboni. From Miss Lovey. From Mitch. From Peanut. Even from Mama. I can stand the heat of Mama on me. Flowing into me. Deep inside to my bones. Even now that it's hot and the fan blow on us. From the floor. Not the window. I like the fan on the floor so the window can be open where I can see. I can stand Mama heart beating soft against my back. And her hands still. Resting. But not moving. I only think Mama be sleeping with me anyway because she don't want to sleep in her own room. Because that's where it happened. Where Imani was killed.

The door to it always be closed now. I heard Mama tell Aunt Mavis on the phone that she has found a place and Mitch moving in with us. Mama don't want to stay, because Imani died here. She only go in her own room to grab some clothes and get out quick. Like she being chased. Like maybe my baby is some ghost. Which I know she ain't.

Even though Imani dead, I can't see her that way. I see her as a living angel up in heaven. Above the trees. Above the Earth and moon and stars. She get a free pass into heaven. Eboni told me. All babies go to heaven. Into the arms of Jesus. He sweep them up to the sky like he they daddy. And I want to hate Jesus. To turn him into the devil. To turn him into the man who killed my baby. But I don't hate him. I'm just jealous. Because I don't know how he get to be with

Imani every day and every night, and I don't. He don't need her more than me. Love her more than me. What Jesus know about singing Imani "Miss Sue from Alabama"? What he know about making her jelly bread the way she like it? Where he going to get punch and red and lemon Kool-Aid and mix them all together and make it sweet for Imani the way she like it? I know heaven supposed to be the best place there is, but when they get some Kool-Aid? And what Jesus know about a black girl hair? I know he ain't got no Royal Crown. He ain't got whole packs of ponytail holders and barrettes. He wasn't here with us long enough to know what to do with a black girl. He was down in his box with his eyes turned to the dark. I think Jesus probably got my baby running around heaven looking like a wilderness angel. With her head all nappy and dry. A dark halo around her head. Like she a state kid somebody took in just for the money. Like she lost.

And she is lost, because she got to be looking for me. Wondering where I'm at in the clouds of heaven. I know she ask for me. All the time. I know she cry, even though I can't hear her. I be listening, but I can't hear her. I know she want for me to bring her home. Her face all ashy with dry tears and no Vaseline to grease it. She wondering why she dead. Do she know? Do she understand that, even coming from Jesus? I don't know how Jesus fix his two lips to tell a baby she been shot to death. How he explain that. Why it had to happen. I don't see how he make it clear to her. But maybe heaven is different from Earth. Maybe heaven is where it make some sense that a baby got shot to death. Because it ain't clear to me down here at the bottom of the dark in the middle of the night.

Maybe all them stars hanging under heaven is answers to

questions asked in heaven. All the things can't nobody understand on Earth. That's why there's so many of them. Maybe God hisself hung a star up there to answer Imani. Maybe he showed his face to her. Looked at her with eyes that looked like they had love in them. Eyes that held her right in they center so he could explain why June Bug had to be at Miss Odetta house like he was. Why he had been staying there for three days when he wasn't even living there no more. I know Mama know. Every cat and dog on the street know whoever shot Imani was gunning for June Bug. If they wasn't, why the next day was he not only gone, but Miss Odetta too? Why, when the sun was big and bold and bright up in the sky, was there a truck backed up right to they front door?

Miss Odetta had just left our house that night. Imani was napping on the couch when she come, so I took my baby upstairs. I ain't take her back to our room. I put her down in Mama room, right on the floor, and closed the door quiet behind her. Then I started cleaning up the kitchen. I was still in there doing the dishes when Miss Odetta left. I was looking out the window. The sky was pretty. It wasn't all the way black. A curve of blue stretched along the top of it above the tops of the dark trees. I was all happy, because school was ending the next day. I'd finished all my exams. Mr. Toliver had even pulled me aside the day before to tell me he had looked at my exam real quick and that I'd done real good. Which meant I would probably get a C for the year. It wasn't a grade he was just giving me. I'd earned it. While I finished the last few dishes, I was thinking all I was going to have to do the next day was turn in my books and clean out my locker. I ain't know if I was going to take Imani with me. It was only going to be a half day.

Mama come into the kitchen then with a dirty ashtray and some glasses and I ask her if I could leave Imani home the next day. Mama say I could.

Right then I was thinking I should go check on Imani. Maybe she was woke. She couldn't get out the room. I went to the bottom of the steps to listen. It was quiet. Nothing but quiet over me, and I should've gone to it. I should've been drawn to it like a vacuum. But I was going up in just a few minutes anyway. All I had was a little bit more dishes to do. What's a few minutes? I was thinking. She sleeping.

And see, Jesus. Why couldn't you look out for me? For Imani when that car turned up our street. Why you let me go back to the sink and scrape some old dried milk out the bottom of Imani bottle with a knife? And let Mama sit down at the table and drink a Pepsi? When you knew that car was coming down our street. That somebody in it had a gun. A nine millimeter. Automatic. And was coming for June Bug.

I was just going to be a few minutes. But, Jesus, why ain't you open up your two lips to say something? Just this one time. Why couldn't you speak to me direct? Instead of sitting back and watch everything happen like it was a movie. Just watching. When you knew my baby was fenna die.

Maybe a star might be enough for my baby. Maybe it can hold the answers to her questions, and she can look down and see it lit up, so she ain't got to ask no more. So she ain't got to bother nobody with her questions. Imani still young. But I got more questions than even God could answer with a whole sky filled with stars. With a whole galaxy. It'll take God, take Jesus, all the time there ever was, there ever will be, to explain why my baby had to die like that when I'm the one to blame.

When the night's deep. When I been at the bottom of the

dark too long, I know Imani ain't die because I put her in Mama room that night. She died because of me, because of me wishing what I did on her birthday. I wished that God would punish *him*. I wished him dead. And now God's punished me.

Derrick Givens. That's his name. Now I can say it in my mind. Taste it in my mouth without having to spit. I can lay next to Mama and cry in the night, saying his name in my mind with another wish in my mouth. Asking Jesus. Telling Jesus. I take it back.

I ain't really want for Derrick to die. I just wanted him gone from my mind. Clean gone. Clear gone. Like my mind that of a baby. Just to not have him be part of Imani life.

I ask Jesus. I say, Jesus, I wish I could go back in time. Let me go back. Let me be the one to die. I'm the one should've been killed. Not my baby. Let me have just one minute to go up them steps. To go into the vacuum of silence and never come back out. Send that car back to the top of the street and let me be up in Mama room with Imani where I can see the car coming. Quiet. With the lights turned off and the music turned off. Moving like a piece of the night. Moving like a animal. A monster coming for me. I would know. I'd recognize it. See what was coming, and push Imani down. Because the police say she was probably at the window. She'd climbed up on the bed and must've been looking out the window. My baby always wanted to see out into this world like there was something for her to see. But, Jesus, I can see in my mind nights. With my eyes turned in, I can see me in Mama room that night. See me knock Imani down. Knock her down so hard I take the breath from her. Just for a minute. So she not hit by the bullet that come through Mama window. Or by the two that come through the living room window. The three that hit the front door. Let one of them hit me. Take me out the world. And I will go without a sound.

But Jesus act like he don't hear me. He just leave me stuck with that night. How things really happened.

Miss Odetta house got hit first. I heard a shot that sounded like it was out the back, over round the way where Peanut live, and I looked out the dark window and thought of him real quick. Hoping he was down his basement. Then I heard another and another real quick. Pop pop. Like firecrackers. I turned to look at Mama just as our living room window was hit. Oh, God, no! Mama screamed. Get down, Tasha!

All I could think about was Imani. My feet took off running. Automatic. My feet carried me into the living room. I called out her name while Mama was screaming behind me and bullets steady hitting our house. Glass was breaking, and I called out for Imani again. Imani, answer me! She ain't answer and my feet moved faster. Taking the steps two at a time. Three at a time. By the time I got to the top, the bullets stopped, and for a few seconds there was nothing but quiet. I ain't pray. I should've started asking you, Jesus, right then. Before I run into Mama room.

The lights was off and I ain't even see Imani down on the floor where I put her. Her blanket was there. I had to turn on the lights to see her. Face down. On the floor over by the dresser. Blood blood blood was pouring from her, so much the rug was wet under her. So much that I ain't see at first. For a second. For a minute. I don't know. But I didn't see that the top of her head was gone. Just gone. Bone and brain. Just gone. There was a hole there. Pulsing with blood. Filling with blood that spilled out onto the rug. I should've prayed then to you, Jesus. Because I fell right to my knees. Screaming. Filling up all the air in the house. I should've stayed right by Imani side. Give her CPR. I remembered what Mrs. Poole taught about saving a baby life. How to cover the nose. How to breathe into the mouth. How to count. How to pump the chest. Gentle but firm. But I knew none of that wasn't going to do no good. I knew right then. When I seen her brain. Imani was dead, and I couldn't stay in that room. Stay in the house.

I took off running. Down them steps. Knocking Mama out the way who was on her way up. Slamming her into the wall while she tried to hold on to me. Saying, God, no! Oh, please God, no. Tasha. Mama say while I was out the door and into the night. No shoes. Just in my sweats. Running like I was crazy. Running like I was wild. My braids flying all around me. Running past Miss Odetta heading for our house in her housecoat. Running past June Bug jumping in his car. My mouth still screaming. Screaming. Screaming. Filling up all the air in the street. All the air in the world. Telling every-body all the way from here to heaven that Imani was dead. I kept on running. Out in the middle of the street. Like I was in a dream. Not even knowing where I was going. I kept run-ning while June Bug flew past me in his car. While I was steady screaming. Telling all the birds in the wilderness. Hid-ing in the dark. In the trees. Calling them all to me. I kept on running to the end of the block. Thinking if I kept going, if I kept running, I could get out this nightmare. That's what it had to be, and I was trapped inside. Maybe Mama could find me deep inside this dream, deep inside this night, and come light the way out.

Because nothing was real to me. The people on our street.

Moving past me. Going the other way. Running the other way. Calling to me. Reaching out they hands to me. Like they was ghosts. Like they was shadows haunting me. It was like I ain't know none of them. I couldn't put a face to none of them. A name to none of them. They wasn't at all real. I just had to keep running. Down our street that was getting darker. Long like some tunnel I was closed inside of. It stretched out longer in front of me the faster I run. But I knew as long as I kept going, Imani would be alive, laying next to me in my bed.

I had got to the end of the street when I passed out. I don't remember even doing it. I was just running. Then I was in the grass of the lady yard who keep her cockeye grandson. Laying in a pile of weeds. Looking up at red and blue lights circling in the dark and faces crowded around me. Sirens was going off all over the place. Somebody say for everybody to get back so I could breathe. I could breathe. And that little boy come and threw a pot of cold water in my face. His grandma slapped him. I don't know how long I was out for. A second. A minute.

I don't know what happened to the time. What happen to time when you slip out of it? Where do it go? Did my Imani slip right out of the world without even knowing what happened? Without any pain?

I sat up and tried to get up. But that old lady say I shouldn't, because one of my feet was cut bad. Cut deep. I don't know when I cut it. How I cut it. It ain't hurt, not one bit. I got up anyway, not sure where to go, when I seen Mama push into the crowd. Push her face right where I could see it. There wasn't no reason for me to run no more. Mama was there, and I knew I wasn't dreaming. I could see on her face. Kin to mine, wild like mine, that everything happening was real.

She say, Tasha, Imani going to be all right. A ambulance coming. She say that to me. Her clothes wet wet with blood. Her hands with blood on them. I could see it. Even in the dark. Wet and darker than the night. Mama had two cops with her. Real dark. Even in the night. Young like boys. But with strong hands like men. Big hands. One got me under one arm. And the other on the other. Mama was holding on to one arm too. Tight tight. She say, Imani arms and legs was moving. I seen for myself. That's good. She can still move. You got to be strong for Imani. She need you strong. You hear me?

I ain't say nothing. Not nam word. I guess the birds had swooped down on me when I was out, pecked my mouth clean. Mama dug her nails hard into my arm. I felt them enter me. Cut right into the flesh of me without no pain. Mama say again that I needed to be strong. It ain't make no difference what Mama say. I could feel Imani death all up inside of me. Heavy like lead.

Latin name, *Plumbum*. It had been on my Latin test that morning.

Mama say, You hear me, Tasha? I heard her. Them hands dragging me along. My feet hardly touching the ground. Three police cars was in front our house. They sat me in back of one of them. Cops was everywhere. Searching all around our house and Miss Odetta house with flashlights. A whole bunch of people. Faces I couldn't really see was gathered behind police tape. Roped behind it. Blue and red lights showing me who they was and then hiding they faces in the night.

Watching me. Watching Mama. Like we was in some kind of show. Look like all the lights was on in our house and I could see heads behind the curtains of Mama room. Moving like ghosts.

Mama was trying to get inside, but they wouldn't let her. She say, I want to see my baby. But they say she couldn't go back in. A ambulance was coming. The biggest cop who helped me home, the darkest one, told me his name. Which went right in and out my head. He took hold of one of my hands and kept talking. I seen then he had on gloves. The kind you wear when you giving a relaxer. He was telling me everything was going to be all right. He say wasn't no need to tell me not to worry. Because he'd worry if he was me. But he say he praying for help. He ask if I want to pray with him. I ain't think he was supposed to even ask me that.

I should've prayed to you then, Jesus. I don't know if he started praying to hisself. I started shaking. More and more. I ain't really feel cold. But I couldn't stop shaking, and he started looking around like my shaking was making him nervous. He kneeled down right by the open door of the car and took both my hands in his. I kept right on shaking. He ain't let go until the ambulance come screaming up the street, and he went away.

All the attendants ran inside and a white man who I think say he was a detective come over to talk to me. I was looking up at Mama window. At all the people inside. Moving around like shadows. The detective say he just want to ask me some questions. What I seen. Who I think could've done the shooting and why. Did I know anybody who owned a dark Trooper. Mama was standing by the car. She had on clothes I never seen before. I guess somebody give them to her to wear.

Mama looked over at the crowd. Then she wasn't there. I heard somebody scream. Hey, hey! Stop her! I tried to get up. The detective told me to sit down.

A cop tried to grab Mama. Mama was too quick. She seen what I seen. Miss Odetta. Mama flew up in the air and landed on top of Miss Odetta. They fell in the grass, and Mama got in some punches and kicks before a cop pulled her off. Still screaming. Still kicking. I'll kill you! Mama screamed. You goddamn bitch. It was you. Your son. Ya'll did this.

Miss Odetta say, Ya'll heard her threaten me. Ya'll heard her. I ain't done nothing. My child ain't done nothing. I'm pressing charges. Arrest her. Arrest her! She crazy, Miss Odetta was shrieking.

The cop who had been talking to me put Mama in the back of the car with me. He say, I know you're upset, but we can't have this. This isn't helping the situation. You're upset. I don't want to cuff you and take you in. Quiet tears was coming down Mama face.

The cop say, You've got to stay in control. For Imani.

Mama nodded. She say, But you just don't understand. You don't understand that's my baby up there.

I reached my hand out to Mama and she held it. Tight.

The detective was still standing outside the car. Mama leaned over me and say, I already told you they was shooting for that nigger next door. June Bug. Everybody know. He stay on the west side. That bitch Odetta ain't going to tell you. But everybody know. Listen to me, Mama say. Find him.

The detective told Mama he had already heard her. He want to know what I had to say.

I ain't say nothing. I closed my eyes. Hoping to find that

dark space again. Slip into that empty space where there wasn't room enough even for time. When I come back, Mama was hollering my name. The detective was gone and one of them ambulance attendants come to look at my foot. It ain't hurt. It was still bleeding, though, and the attendant say it wasn't bad, but I needed stitches. He ask whose child Imani was, and I say mine. He say, She's alive, and they're preparing to bring her out any minute. He say no family was riding with her to the hospital. We could stand behind the police tape if we want to see her come out.

Mama grabbed my hand. Decided for me. I let her and that cop who'd been with me come back to my side and help me stand up. While the space of night around us lit up like the day. Not just one sun, but three rose over our heads. Lights on television cameras. Pointing right at us. I don't know when they come. But I put my head down. Just that quick, they carried Imani past us strapped on a stretcher. She went by so fast. Surrounded by so many people, I couldn't even see her.

Me and Mama went right behind her in a cop car. Racing to ECMC. Sirens going. Lights flashing. The big dark cop was driving, while me and Mama sat in the back. I looked over at Mama but turned my face away. I ain't want to see the wildness of her face no more. The fear that had her rocking on the seat next to me. Folding and unfolding her hands like they was going in and out of prayer. I watched out the window. Looking past my own face at the ambulance speeding ahead of us.

They took Imani right into emergency and took me to get my foot stitched up. This young black woman did it. She gave me a shot. She smiled, but she ain't say much to me. I don't know if somebody told her. About Imani. So she wouldn't be making no small talk. Asking how I cut my foot. Telling me the shot wasn't going to hurt one bit. Letting me know how many stitches she was putting in. She just worked, and when she finished, she told me to not put pressure on my heel and to shower with it in a plastic bag for the next two days.

Then she let me go to Mama, who was sitting in the waiting room. So was Mitch. I don't know when Mama called him. He had his work uniform on and he wiped his tears away when he seen me, rushed right up to me, and pulled me tight to him. He kept saying over and over, I'm so sorry, darling. I'm so sorry. I'm so sorry.

I sat down next to Mama. Mama was steady rocking. Mitch sat still. His face red red. His eyes swollen. Mama was talking soft to him. Saying, Imani going to make it. My baby going to be all right. Mitch ain't say nothing. He was praying. Steady praying with his hands pressed together. His lips moving. While I listened to the fluorescent lights hum and watched the hands of the waiting room clock sail slow around its face.

Almost a hour went by before a nurse come and ask us to come with her. Mama jumped right straight up out her chair. How's Imani? Mama ask.

The nurse say, The doctor will talk to you.

Mama started moaning. She knew. I think we all knew. The nurse put us in a small room with no windows. It was cold in there.

When this short, white doctor come in to talk to us with his hands balled up in his pockets and his eyes on the floor, he really ain't have to say what he say. He sat down right next to me and say, We did all we could.

Mama moaned even louder, and tears come down her face.

All of a sudden it seemed like Mama nerves took hold of her. They took over her hands. Her hands started fluttering out in front of her like they was trying to fly away from her body, and Mama fell back in her chair. Hollering. Mitch grabbed hold of her. But Mama fought against him. Her hands beating him. The doctor looked at the floor. I stared at him hard, so hard I think it made him look up. He looked like he want to leave. But he sat there until Mama calmed down. She was still moaning. Still crying. I wasn't crying. Because I already knew. Mama was the one who was hoping. The one who had prayers in her hands, even though she has never said she did. Mitch had both of his arms wrapped around Mama. Holding her hands close to her body.

The doctor say, Imani didn't suffer. You should know that. If you'd like to see her. To have some private time. You can. But I'll caution you, you might not want to see her in the condition she's in. I'll leave it up to you. He got up and left.

Mitch say, I'll go see Imani, and I'll decide if you should see her.

Mama started fighting against him again. She say, I'm going to see my baby! You ain't deciding a goddamn thing for nobody. Mitch let Mama go. She jumped up and say, I'm the one doing the deciding.

I say. Soft. Mitch can decide for me.

Mama looked at me. Like I'd slapped her. She ain't say nothing.

Mitch say Mama could go first while he waited with me.

Mama say, No, you go on. Tasha say she want you to go for her, so, damn it, go.

Mitch just say, All right. And he left the room. Mama

moved next to me and I held her hands. They was cold. Empty of prayers.

When Mitch come back, I knew I ain't want to see Imani. I seen him shift me from the center of his eyes. Hold me off to the side. He ain't say nothing. If he'd opened his mouth, I think he would've cried. Mama seen how he looked, but she went to see Imani anyway while I sat with Mitch and he put his arms around me. Like a daddy. Even though I'm past having a daddy.

Later that night when we went out to Mitch house, and I was laying on the couch, I heard Mama tell Mitch she wish she hadn't seen Imani. They was sitting in the kitchen, talking quiet. She ain't say why she wished it. But I knew.

I listened to the two of them crying all night. Talking all night. They voices flashing in and out. Close to me. Hanging low in the dark like fireflies. Then far far away. Like starlight. I couldn't cry like them. Hard. Deep down to my bones. Only regular tears come from me. Soft. Tears not at all crazy. But sane, and running down my face onto my neck. Tickling my neck the way Peanut lashes do. They only come when I think about Imani being alone. Not nowhere with Jesus. Not halfway from here to heaven. But alone. All by herself in the bottom on the night.

I ain't even think I'd slept until the next morning, when I heard Aunt Mavis nem coming in the door. I'd been in that timeless space again that ain't seem at all like sleep. I opened my eyes, and it was bright. Aunt Mavis held on to me for too long. I had to let her go, because I could feel her heart beating all fast against me. Racing. If I had stayed pressed up against her, I ain't know where it would've took me.

I went out the back and sat on the deck. Junior come right

behind me. He had on sunglasses, early as it was, and he kept shaking his head. It's messed up. The whole thing is messed up, he keep saying. He was sipping on a pop. My mouth was dry, and I ask him for a sip. He say, Ain't hardly none left.

I snatched the bottle from him. Don't be stingy, I say. I took a big swallow and spit it out.

Junior say, Look at you. Wasting my stuff.

I say, What is this?

He say, You know what it is.

I ain't. It was some liquor, I knew that much.

He say, It take the edge off. I got more if you need it.

I ain't say nothing.

He say, You might before everything is over.

Shoot, I need it now, Junior say.

Frankie come out the house. He had a pop, too. I ask for a sip. He wiped off the top on his shirt and handed it right to me. It was warm and all pop. He sat down right up under me on the next step. Where's Imani? he ask.

Junior say, Shut up, you big head. Why you got to go ask something like that?

Frankie say, Because I want to know.

Junior say, Daddy told you don't be asking a bunch of questions.

I say, It's all right. She still in the hospital.

Frankie say, Mama say she in heaven. How can she be in the hospital and in heaven at the same time?

I say, I don't know.

Frankie ask, How long do it take to get to heaven? Can you get all the way up there quick? He lay his head back in my lap and pointed up at the sky. His mouth was filling with big teeth now. Square and white, with spaces in between. Two still missing on the sides.

Junior took a drink and say, Maybe Superman took her.

Frankie say, Don't you say that. You being stupid. Superman don't take people to heaven. I kissed Frankie on the top of his head. I don't know why. But I did, and he ain't wipe it off. He say, Imani got her own wings to fly. She a angel. For real.

It was after noon before we all got showered and dressed. I ain't have no shoes. No clothes but the sweats I wearing. They had dirt on them. Blood on them. On the pants. Brown. I don't know if it was my blood or Imani blood. Junior let me wear some of his sweats and a pair of his sneakers. The sneakers was big on me, which was good, because my foot was hurting some. I didn't cover it in the shower and it was throbbing pain up my leg. Every time my heart beat, I felt another pulse.

All morning long Mama nem had been making phone calls. They was all set to leave me and the boys at Mitch house, because Uncle Willis say they had to make arrangements. I say I want to go and so did the boys.

Mama ask, You sure you want to go back to the house?

I say I was, and all them looked at me. Out the corner of they eyes. But in two cars, we went. I rode with Aunt Mavis nem. Mitch with Mama.

As we drove down our street, I looked out the car window and seen heads turning. Like they was waiting for us. The little boy who'd throwed that water in my face the night before seen us and raced us to the house, still circled in police tape. And out in front of our house was something that made us all take a breath.

On the sidewalk was a memorial. People had come and put stuffed animals and flowers and cards and even some balloons tied to a light pole.

Frankie ask, What's all this stuff for? Ain't nobody answer him.

Seeing all them things made it easier for me to get out the car. I was thinking Imani will like this. It was so pretty. Like a party.

The little boy who was racing us come up to me. He say, Peanut looking for you. He say for me to tell you.

Frankie say, Imani my cousin. And the boy took off running again.

Mama nem was looking through all the things, and I started looking, too. All of the stuffed animals was new except this one. A teddy bear that was all nubby and dirty. It had a card tied around its neck with a ribbon. I opened it. It was a sympathy card somebody had wrote. *You don't know us or our daughter Jennifer, but this is her favorite bear. She wanted Imani to have it.*

There was money in the card, and Mama took it from my hand. She started collecting all the cards and piling the toys in Frankie arms. But I ask Frankie to leave the toys there. Mama say for me to suit myself, but they might get stole.

Frankie ask, Can I put a toy here for Imani?

I told him he could and he dropped the animals and went to the car. Everybody else went in, and I waited for Frankie to come back with a plastic Superman that looked like it was flying. He got down on his knees, arranged all the animals in two neat rows, and put his Superman right in the front. So Imani can see it, he say.

We ducked under the police tape, and soon as we got in the house, the phone was ringing. Mama answered it and I went to change into my own clothes. The door to Mama room was open. I ain't go in, but I peeked. Newspaper was down on the floor where Imani fell. Wet and dark with big brown stains and traces of orange and yellow seeping through. I felt like I'd throw up, and I wanted to leave not just our house but the whole world. I don't know why I thought the room would be cleaned.

Frankie grabbed hold of my hand. You OK, Tasha? You want for me to get Mama? I told him no and he led me like I was some child into my room. He sat with me while I changed and maybe I should've been shamed in front of him, but I wasn't. I was glad he was there. Watching over me. I even changed my drawers while he sat on the bed holding one of Imani dolls. The phone rang again, and I heard a bunch of feet on the stairs.

Junior knocked and pushed the door right open, without asking if he could come in. Peanut, Eboni, Kente, and Coco was all with him. They all hugged me tight. Crying. Frankie punched on the radio and somebody was rapping about the thug life while Junior was steady sipping. Steady taking the edge off hisself.

Uncle Willis come up and say he needed some help, and all the boys went off with him. Even Frankie. Eboni say there was plenty of food if I want to eat. Miss Lovey had cooked all night. She'd seen Imani on the news. Seen me and Mama, and they been calling and calling and calling the house. Miss Lovey couldn't sleep, and Eboni say she stayed up with her. They made macaroni and cheese. Buffalo wings. Fried chicken. Tuna and macaroni salad. A pound cake and a jelly cake.

Eboni say her and Coco came over first thing in the morning with the food, hoping me and Mama was back, and when wasn't nobody home, they went to Peanut house. Coco say,

Peanut ain't even know. He was on his way to school, and she and Eboni told him. He stayed home. Eboni say I should eat. Coco say I should eat. They would make me a plate. Coco say she would get it. My mouth should've been watering for Miss Lovey food. But it wasn't. I ate. I could've even ate the plate without knowing it.

We all spent the rest of the day with the radio playing soft out in the backyard inside the shade of the trees with they hands still like babies. Eboni jumped up to turn it off the first time the news come on and they talked about Imani. I told her to leave it. They say it was a senseless tragedy and they ain't have no leads in the drive-by shooting. It ain't last but a few seconds no way. Then they talked about the weather.

Uncle Willis and Mitch and the boys was working hard in the house. They got a carpet cleaner. Replaced windows and screens. They even did laundry. Scrubbed the kitchen. Cleaned the bathroom. While the phone kept ringing and from time to time Frankie come to us to rest for a few minutes and tell us what was going on. There was more toys out front, and he was keeping them straight. People was bringing food and more food. They was running out of places to put it all.

He say, I had Buffalo wings and two kinds of cake. Later, he say there's a moving truck next door pulled right up to the porch. He looked all excited in a strange kind of way when he told us the news cameras had been out front. Eboni and Coco raced to see them. But Frankie say they was gone. He say Uncle Willis told the reporters they couldn't talk to me, and I was glad he decided. I ain't want to be on the news. Frankie say, Daddy let them see Imani picture.

Which one? I ask.

She got on a purple dress, Frankie say.

Mama and Aunt Mavis was gone almost all day. When they got back, they come out to the backyard. They faces was pinched shut like they was holding in more than they was telling. Peanut was sitting next to me on the stoop, with Frankie sitting right up under me. I thought Frankie was going to sit in Aunt Mavis lap when she come, but he was shamed to on account of the big boys, so he sat next to her. Junior sat way off on a lawn chair almost at the side of the house. He was way past drunk, I know. Still sitting with sunglasses on and drinking from a pop bottle. Eboni and Coco fixed plates for Mama and Aunt Mavis, and they picked and talked.

Mama say they had been to the welfare. But the welfare ain't give enough money to bury somebody in a cardboard box, let alone a casket.

Aunt Mavis say, I told you me and Willis will take care of things.

Mitch say, Me too, Earlene. Darling, don't worry about the money. Everything is going to be taken care of.

Mama and Aunt Mavis had also been to a funeral home. Paterson Brothers. Imani not ready to be released to the funeral home for one more day. When Mama told me that, I went on upstairs.

I thought I might cry, and I ain't want nobody to see. I was thinking about Imani. That she'd spent the day being touched by strangers who ain't know nothing about how I loved her. How could they know? When they seen her like that. And she was going to be alone. Again. In the night. All closed up in a drawer.

But I didn't cry none when I got upstairs. I laid across the bed with my face in a pillow. I could smell Imani in it, and I stayed there until Frankie come up. I'd fell through some hole in time, because it was dark out and it sounded like there was a party going on in the house.

The stereo was on downstairs playing some old seventies song like Uncle Willis nem like, and so many people was talking, they voices all run together in a blur.

Frankie had his arms full of toys he got from out front. Where you want them? he ask. I told him I ain't care, and he put them in the crib. Frankie say, Junior nem say can we come in here? Them mosquitoes eating us up outside. I told him they could.

Kente was the first one through the door. He say, All them old people done took downstairs over.

Coco say, Old people? My mama only thirty-two. Talk about your own mama. She old as hell.

Eboni was going to sit next to me on the bed, but Peanut act like he was crazy. He pushed her all out the way and dove onto the bed next to me.

Eboni say, See you, big head boy, you ain't had no home training. Up in people house tearing up they furniture.

He say, Forget you. This a place I been wanting to get to.

Eboni say, Please, you was just up in here this afternoon.

Peanut say, Not on the bed. If your Mama could see me now, Tasha.

Frankie say, If Aunt Earlene want to see you now, she can just come up here.

Junior was passing his pop bottle around, and Kente, Eboni, Peanut, and Coco took a drink. Coco passed it to me and I took a drink. It was nasty. But when Frankie ask for some, I turned the bottle up to my mouth and drank it all.

Almost a half bottle, and it made my stomach all warm in one instant.

By the time I went to bed, all the edges had been rubbed off me, and I felt all smooth and light. Like I was floating. Like I was walking on water. When I laid down in the bed, with Junior and Frankie on the floor below me, I floated right out the window and off into the night.

I ain't get a chance to be with Imani until three days later, at the wake. We got there early and parked around the back. I ain't want to get out the car.

Mama say, It's all right, Tasha. We all going in with you, and the casket closed. Me and Aunt Mavis seen to that.

But I couldn't go in just then.

Mitch say, Why don't you just wait in the car for a while? Take some time to yourself. It's still early. Somebody will come get you.

Frankie ask, Can I stay with you, Tasha? I'll stay with you.

Junior say, Leave Tasha alone.

I say, He all right. He can stay.

Mitch rolled the windows down.

When they left, Frankie ask me, You scared to see Imani?

I say, We ain't going to see her.

Frankie say, in a soft voice like a baby, I know we ain't really going to see her, but I want to talk to Imani when we go in. Junior say he was going to slap me if I do it. Mama say Imani can hear you all the time even if you talk without moving your lips, because when you get to heaven you get super power hearing.

I say, Aunt Mavis ain't even say that.

Frankie say, Not like I say it, but I'm not telling a story. Want some Red Hots?

I told Frankie I ain't want none, and he poured some in his mouth.

Uncle Willis come back for us soon after that. He took one hand and Frankie the other. Out front the funeral home, so many teenagers was on the sidewalk, it looked like a school had just let out right there. There was a line to go inside. I ain't seen none of my friends, but I seen some of my teachers. Mrs. Poole was standing with Mr. Diaz, my Latin teacher, and these secretaries nem from the office. Two of my teachers from middle school and Mr. Toliver was all standing off to one side.

Mr. Toliver come right over soon as he seen me. He had on sunglasses and he hugged me real hard. I am so sorry, Tasha, he say. His voice all tight. His face all tight like he was going to cry if there was any looseness anywhere in him. Mr. Toliver ask Uncle Willis if he was my daddy. I told him who he was, and Mr. Toliver cleared his throat and went on about me. Tasha is a fine student. A fine girl. If there is anything. Anything I can do. Don't hesitate to call. My number is in the card, he say, and handed a card to Uncle Willis. Uncle Willis thanked him, and we went inside.

Being family, we ain't have to wait. I was surprised the funeral home was so small. There was a entry hall with a church pew full up with people. The main room was painted in this soft pink and lit dim. I counted about seven or eight rows of folding chairs. All filled. Uncle Willis say there was a row saved up front for the family. People was steady coming in around us and leaving around us.

One of the Paterson Brothers introduced hisself to me. He was a short dark man with a half-bald head. His breath smelled like Sen-Sens. He say he would take us all down front. Like we had such a long way to go. But he parted the crowd, which pulled back like a wave. It was hot in the room, like the heat was on, and it was hard for me to breathe. I pulled air into me. But it didn't seem to come in any farther than my mouth. My feet stopped when I seen the tiny white box with Imani picture sitting on top of it.

I let Mama nem decide everything for the funeral except two things. Things I wanted to have because I knew Imani would like them. First, Miss Lovey was going to sing at the funeral. I thought it would be nice for a preacher to speak. The one from Eboni nem church. Mama ain't want that. In a way, Mama was right. That preacher don't know Imani. He ain't bless her. He wouldn't be able to say nothing personal about my baby. But I thought Miss Lovey singing would be personal. The other thing I decided was the dress Imani would wear. The purple one she'd wore for her birthday. Wasn't nobody going to see it. The picture of her wearing it on her birthday was going to be there.

It was the picture that made me stop the night of the wake. It's crazy how you know things and don't know them all at the same time. I knew I was never going to see Imani again from the second I seen her on the floor in Mama bedroom, but until I seen her picture sitting on the coffin, it seem like I ain't really *know* it. The real knowing, the deep-in-my-bones knowing, took the breath from me. Stopped my feet. Uncle Willis and Frankie pulled me along, and my feet moved. Not because I wanted them to. They moved slow and my legs got a weakness in them. A baby step. A baby step. We moved right up to the coffin and passed it. I ain't cast my eyes at it direct. I looked at the floor as we come near it.

Frankie say, Hey, Imani, we here. And Junior reached out

from the front row and slapped Frankie upside his head. Uncle Willis slapped Junior on the shoulder with his free hand.

Junior say, I don't see why you hitting me. Frankie the one said something stupid.

We all sat down while Aunt Mavis say, through her teeth, Stop acting like crazy people in public.

My friends was sitting in the second row. Eboni say, We got here early. We had two extra chairs in the front row, and I ask Peanut and her to come and sit up front with us. Frankie ain't like it when Peanut ask him to slide down. I heard him say, Ya'll ain't no kin to us. But he moved.

I never been to a wake before. I ain't really know what was going to happen. What I was supposed to do. It was two hours of people I knew and ain't know giving me hugs. Crying. Shaking they heads. Rushing by the coffin or stopping to look at Imani picture for a long time. Some people brung toys. Pressed cards into my hands. Touched Frankie on the head when he say, Imani my cousin. Shook Uncle Willis, Junior, Mitch, and Peanut hand. Rocked Mama and Aunt Mavis in they arms. Kissed Eboni on the cheek.

When the night was just about over I heard this sound. This moan coming from the back. Low at first, but louder and louder, until it come out of the throat that held it. A wail. Like a voice long lost in the wilderness. I looked back to see who it was. It was a girl about my age. I ain't know who she was, but she changed the night. Touched the pain right below everybody skin. I could hear more moaning. And more moaning. And cries escaping from the tiny lit room into the dark of the wilderness I could see out a single round window. Mama and Mitch was crying. I could hear them. Knew what they sounded like crying together. Near and far. I ain't cry.

I ain't cry at the funeral neither. Mama fell all apart. She was the one who cried so hard, she couldn't hardly sit up. Mama was the one wailing. She was the one moaning. The one kicking. Aunt Mavis had to hold her up. Mitch had to hold her up. They pressed in close to her, and I sat on the other side of Aunt Mavis. Fanning. Lifting tiny waves of heat off her. That returned and returned.

The closest I come to crying was when Miss Lovey started singing. Miss Lovey words flowed into me. Echoed in me. Shaking me from the inside out.

She sang:

> Why should I feel dis-cour-aged,
> Why should the shad-ows come,
> Why should my heart be lone-ly,
> And long for heav'n and home,
> When Je-sus is my por-tion,
> My cons-tant Friend is He;
> His eye is on the spa-row,
> And I know he watch-es me.

I wanted to hold them words in me. To have them fill me up. But when Miss Lovey finished with the last note, while it was still hanging in the air like a bird, them words had already gone from me. And I was empty.

I laid down that day while there was still blue in the sky and woke up in the dark with Mama laying next to me. Empty. Even with her hands on me. Fearing for me. Worrying for me.

Mama don't know the power in her hands. She think her hands done failed because I don't be talking. That's why she let Eboni come and bring her two twins to our house. I like to hold the girls and smell the tops of they heads. They smell like Imani. Not just they grease but the inside of them I can smell. The greenness of they life. The sweetness.

Mama even let Peanut come to see me in my room. She don't ask me a bunch of questions, neither. She let him come right up the steps. Peanut like it. Mostly me and him talk and listen to music. Maybe Mama know, maybe she don't know. That me and him even done it. Twice. Right in this bed. While she sat downstairs watching TV. I wasn't a woman with Peanut neither time. Just a child with my eyes wide open watching the shadows of trees blowing across the ceiling.

I ain't really talk to Peanut when he was over. I ain't had nothing to say to him. I don't have nothing to say to nobody, even though I know they all still waiting for words to come out of me. But there just ain't none. They was snatched from me the night my baby left this world. Maybe Mama nem think I can just wish them back. But they don't know I wish every night.

With Mama hands on my back, still late in the night, I be looking outside my window at this one lone star hanging in the sky. I been watching it a long while now. How it rise in the dark and slide across the sky into the silver blue of dawn. I keep my eye on it. I hold it in the center of my eye and spend the night wishing for more than I can ever tell them. More than I'll ever be able to say.

ELEVEN

Here Is the Church

I AIN'T SET OUT to come to New Light this morning. My feet brung me. They carried me there when I left the house. Like they knew it was where I should be. Like they knew more than my mind. All I was wanting to do was get out the house. We moving today. I don't want to be home for that. To see how me and Imani lives can be carried away in such small boxes.

Mama ask me this morning, Where you think you going with all this work to do?

Mitch say, Let her go, Earlene. We can manage.

Not nam other word came out Mama mouth. She threw her hands up and walked away from me.

Mama disgusted with me, anyway. My name been bitter in her mouth ever since I told her I'm pregnant. She ask me the same thing she ask me when I was pregnant with Imani. You happy now?

I don't know why Mama even ask me that. She not happy now. I hear her some nights before she come to bed with me. She be with Mitch downstairs. Crying. She try to do it soft.

To not let me hear. But I hear. Because it's a crying filled with craziness. A crying that take hold of you and don't let go until it's through with you. Until you empty.

I looked once. Just once. They was sitting close up on each other on the couch. And I seen both of they faces in the dark. For the first time I seen in Mama face that she love Mitch. Her face was like a full moon. From where Mitch was sitting, he couldn't see it. I don't know if Mama ever show that face to him. The one I seen. But maybe Mitch know Mama love him. Maybe he can hear it in her when they all alone and he find the secret place in her that is small small small. A place open just for him.

Mama know I ain't happy. There ain't nothing that look like happiness in me. Maybe that's why, when she ask me, she ain't slap me like she did when I told her about Imani. Mama ain't lift a hand to me in love or hate. She be acting like I done slapped her, though. Sent her tumbling into my future, where she don't see no dream she have for me coming true. Mama ain't got no more dreams for me. This baby has took them all away.

I was past tired this morning when I got to church because I had walked and walked. Without thinking about how far I was going. If I knew where I was going, I could've just got on the bus. But I ain't know. My feet was leading me through the streets where folks was washing cars, sitting on they porches, going into corner stores, barbecuing, climbing the steps of churches. I went past dealers. Some of them leaned up against buildings like they was tired, and I seen some of they clients. Them gray zombies looking like they wasn't going in no real direction.

And kids. I passed by so many of them. Little girls ready

for church wearing dresses with lace, ribbons flying in they hair. Boys in dress pants and shirts, ties knotted like big fists at they skinny necks. Little girls and boys ready to do nothing but play. They was on almost every block with they jump ropes and they jacks and they hopscotches done in chalk. With they bikes and they balls and skates. With girls singing and clapping they hands to the same songs I used to and boys arguing about what they was arguing about when I was little. Who was out, who was in, who was tagged, who was safe.

I ain't even notice the sun was getting higher and higher in the sky. Pouring heat into my head. I knew I needed to stop because I was seeing spots. Tiny little worlds was spinning around in front of me when I heard music. Soft music rolling up the sidewalk. Just the edges of it. Creeping in on me. Cool on my feet. And my feet followed it. Wanting what was in the middle of the music. Wanting what was on the other side of it.

Eboni and Miss Lovey been trying to get me to come to church with them. They both ask me since the funeral, but I told them I ain't feel like it. Neither one of them could get me to do what my feet did this morning.

As I stepped inside the cool cool church, I was struck blind by the darkness of it. It's darker than I remembered. Thick with bodies blocking out the light. The wholeness of the organ music hit me full in the chest and I felt myself falling back. Falling like I was heading out of time. A flash of white come up alongside of me. A usher. She caught me up under the arm to show me to a seat. I wasn't going to let her lead me. Not one step. Because I wasn't staying. I wasn't dressed to sit with them people. I had on shorts and a T-shirt. But my feet moved on. Past rows of benches. Past the moon overhead and the man in it. All the way to the front, where I could see the preacher clear.

He was dressed in a long black robe trimmed in gold and already wiping sweat from his face like he was hot. Like he been preaching a long time. He waved his hands and the music stopped. Sudden. Taking the church into a quiet place. Taking me there, too, while the preacher started out talking in a soft voice about waiting on the Lord.

He say, I'm not going to keep ya'll here all day. My time is running short. My time is winding up, but I can't let you go just yet. The Lord won't let me let you go just yet. Not until *I* tell you. Not until I *tell* you. Not until I tell *you*. About waiting. On him. He want you to stay. He want you to wait. I'm not the one who asking you to wait. It's nothing but the Lord.

The preacher say he going to read out the book of Isaiah. Chapter forty. Verse thirty-one. He say turn and find that passage. A old lady who was bald on top of her head shared her Bible with me. She let it rest part on my lap and part on hers. I ain't look in it as the preacher read:

> But they that wait upon the Lord shall renew their strength; they shall mount up with wings as eagles; they shall run, and not be weary; and they shall walk, and not faint.

The preacher say, You know, church. We a waiting people. We a people who will wait on anything. He say if we ain't believe him, go past a check-cashing center on a payday. Go by there on the first or fifteenth of the month. He say, Line be out the door. It be raining, snowing, sleeting, hailing. But ya'll wait. Am I lying?

No, say the voices. We wait.

Church, we going to *wait* on some money. Let that Lotto

jackpot hit ten million dollars, and watch out, the preacher say, getting loud. He ducked down and jumped back up. I say, watch out now. Ya'll folk forget about the street number. Ya'll forget about the Pick Three, Pick Four. Ya'll ain't thinking about what to play straight. What to box. What to knick-knack patty-whack. Ya'll going to wait in that Lotto line. I'm telling you, *Jez-us* could come back, and ya'll wouldn't get out the line to see him. Some of ya'll might slap him if he tried to bogart ahead of you. Am I lying?

The dark answered, You telling the truth. You preaching.

The preacher wiped his face, his neck. Ya'll with me. Stay with me. Stay with me, sisters, because I know some of you out there waiting. On some man. On some half a man. To treat *you* right. And you, brothers, too. Some of ya'll waiting on some trifling woman. To treat *you* right. Ya'll *wait* on somebody to change. Wait your whole life. But you won't spend one second waiting on the Lord. Anybody got a Amen to that?

Amen, Preacher! Amen!

We a people, see. We a people. I tell you about Moses. I tell you about the Israelites. In bondage. In Egypt. In the wilderness. Them folk wandered. Forty years. And I can hear what some of ya'll be thinking. You don't think I do, but I do. Ya'll be thinking, Ha! That couldn't have been me. Them folks. They had to be crazy. Them folks. Well, they must've been white. Them folks. They must've ain't had nothing else to do. Waiting out in the wilderness. You thinking, I wouldn't have waited forty minutes. Because, well, you know. I got some money waiting on me. I got a man waiting on me. I got woman waiting on me. I ain't got time to be waiting on the Lord. The Lord should be waiting on me.

And you want the Lord to *wait* on you. To serve you. To

give you what you need. What you want. And if he don't, then watch this. This here what you do, he say.

The preacher turned around. Turned his eyes away. Turned his face away from the church. I was fenna get up to leave then. Without him seeing me. Duck down and walk quick up the aisle. Because I'd heard enough. But before I could move, he spun back around.

I know ya'll sometimes. Lord. More than I know myself. I know your minds. Lord. More than I know my own. I know what you thinking when you think. Lord. My father done let me down. My mama. She done let me down. My children. Done let me down. My husband. He ain't no good. My wife. She ain't no good. My life. It's done let me down. My life. Is not the life I want. This life. Is not the life I asked for. And you say, Lord. Lord, I'm weary. Lord, I'm worn. Lord, I'm tired. And the Lord say, Wait!

Just wait on me. Not on some money. Lord say, Wait! But not on some man. Lord say, Wait! And I *will* lift you up. I will mount you up with wings as eagles. How many of you need to be lifted up this morning?

All around me voices called out. They answered him. Lift me up, Lord. Yes, Jesus. Yes, Lord. Yes, Lord. The music slipped in under they voice with its own voice. Deep. Worrying.

How many of you this morning need the Lord to renew you? So you can keep on walking through that wilderness?

I need you, Lord. I need you. I need you, Jesus.

How many of you need the strength to run and not get weary? To walk and not faint? To go into the wilderness in these streets? In your neighborhood. Round your block. And have the strength to walk. To run forty years if you have to without doubting how. Without doubting. Why. Them Israelites done it.

They did it because they knew. They knew. I say, they knew. What Paul knew. They knew. What Paul say. They knew. Before he said it. They knew. Before he was born. They knew. What he told the Corinthians. When he say *For we walk by faith, not by sight.*

I'm not talking about the walking you do with your feet, the preacher say. He walked halfway up the aisle and back to the front of the church.

That's ordinary walking. The walking a baby can do. A child can do. I'm talking about the walking you do in yourself. The walking you do all deep down in your soul. By yourself and with yourself. And if you not walking by faith this morning, then maybe you don't know the Lord. You don't know. What he can do for you. You don't know. What he has done for you.

I stood up then. Not caring who seen me. I stood right up in front the preacher. With tears running down my face. I wasn't crying, but tears was coming from me. I ain't care what the preacher say. I ain't care what the music say. The Lord ain't know me, and I ain't want to know him.

I went to turn my back on him. To turn my back on God. But my feet ain't take nam other step. They kept me standing in front of him. While the preacher say right to my face. While he say looking me right in the center of my eyes. *Be still, and know that I am God.* That's all you got to do. Be still.

But I wanted to move, because I could feel that music rising. I could feel it worrying me deep inside. Where there was a stillness in me. Deep in the dark of me. While them tears kept coming.

Somebody started singing, It's me, it's me, it's me, O Lord, standing in the need of prayer. It's me, it's me, it's me, O Lord, standing in the need of prayer.

Everybody started singing. They voices filling the church. Filling up all the spaces that wasn't filled by the benches. That wasn't filled by they bodies. They wasn't filled by the music.

> Not my brother, not my sister, not the preacher,
> not the deacon, not my father, not my mother,
> not a stranger, not my neighbor
> But it's me, O Lord, standing in the need of prayer.

They just kept on. Clapping. It's me. Singing. It's me. Clapping. It's me.It's me. It's me.It's me. It's me.It's me. Until they words made they way deep inside me and I started crying. Out loud. My mouth wide open. The old woman standing next to me touched me and I tried to pull away. I ain't see Eboni or Miss Lovey. I wanted them to come to me. To save me from what I was feeling. Like I was being carried off from myself, and I wanted Mama next to me. Because I couldn't pull away from this old lady who ain't know me. From these people who ain't know me. People who I was shame in front of. Crying. Screaming. With my mouth all open. With my tongue saying words I could hear but didn't know.

That old woman ain't let me loose, and I was starting to feel like I ain't want her to. I could smell in her a sweetness. Stronger than any promise before rain. I wanted her there. Wanted her to hold me right where I was. I needed her hands on me. Needed that circle of people that had formed around me. Laying they hands on me. Standing all around me. Thick and dark. Strong like trees. Strong like the dark. Closing me up in they arms. I needed them watching over me.

With no shame in me, I fell down to my knees. And I ain't

care who saw me. Who heard me cry. I wanted them to hear me. To listen to all I had to say. Even if my mind was confused. If my tongue was confused. And I couldn't understand myself. The sounds coming from me like cries of a bird. I let them come out of me, and the more they came out, the more I knew what I knew. Somewhere inside me.

I knew Imani wasn't killed because of me. I seen that clear in the stillness inside of me. Black like night as I felt myself being pulled clear out of myself and pulled back in. I seen a bird. White like snow. Rise up out the dark. Fly up in the air and disappear.

And I made up my mind right then. Down on that floor with them people around me. With they hands touching me. With they hands loving me. With the music flowing over me like water. I made up my mind that I want the baby inside me.

The baby calling me. Calling me into the stillness in me. The dark in me. Loving me right then. And I loved it right then.

I'm not keeping this baby a secret from nobody. I'm not keeping it a secret from myself, hid away from myself. It's growing right where Imani did.

I ain't told Peanut about the baby yet. I want to tell him to his face. I am going to look him right in his eyes. Direct. And I want to see if that's the way he'll look at me. If he will conceive of this baby with me. If he will love both of us. If he will hold us in the center of his eyes. Or slide us to the far corner, where we slip out of his sight altogether.

I don't care what Mama say about this baby and me. I'm having this baby. This baby being in me is bringing me back to Imani a step at a time. A minute at a time.

One day I'm going to feel this baby heart beating inside

me. Just like with Imani. And a sweetness will come to my mouth. Fill my mouth. Like it do when I say Imani. When I say her name. Like I did today in that church when I was done down on that floor. When I was empty and I was filled. And them people helped me up. Helped me rise and walk. Like I was walking on water. Like Jesus touched my hand. Like I have a faith that's all mine.

All-Bright Court and *Imani all Mine*
by Connie Porter

All-Bright Court

In the upstate New York mill town of Lackawanna, the company-built housing project known as All-Bright Court represents everything its residents have dreamed of—jobs, freedom, and a future. The outcome of those dreams is the stuff of Connie Porter's acclaimed debut novel. Through twenty years, as the promises of the 1960s give way to hardship and upheaval, Porter chronicles the loves, hopes, troubles, triumphs, and ambitions of Mississippi-born Sam and Mary Kate Taylor and their neighbors. As the late 1970s fade the Court's bright colors and a people's optimism, young Mikey Taylor—gifted, ambitious, and proud—comes to embody an entire community's dreams and disappointments.

FOR DISCUSSION

1. Porter has said that in this novel "the reader can see the impact of the political life of this country on a group of people." What impact do the major events and issues in American "political life" have on the people of All-Bright Court? How are some of these political and social issues still important?

2. What arguments do the characters present for *and* against playing by the white man's rules—for example: getting an education, paying taxes, working hard? In what circumstances are those arguments voiced? What are the desired and actual results of each way of acting? In what ways do the same arguments apply today for black Americans, Hispanic Americans, and Asian Americans?

3. In chapter 8, Porter writes that Moses "hid within the shell of his words. They were a way of protecting him from the truth." How and why do various characters use words both to hide from the truth and to express or expose the truth? How is it that language may be used for both purposes?

4. Porter writes, "It was Samuel who challenged" what Mary Kate knew and thought she knew; he "challenged who she thought she was." In what ways does Sam challenge his wife's view of herself? What are the consequences of Sam's challenge? What additional challenges—emotional, intellectual, and social, for example—are pre-

sented to the characters by one another? What are the outcomes of those challenges?

5. What southern country ways, habits, and beliefs do the people of All-Bright Court retain? Why? How do these habits and beliefs help these people cope with the demands and circumstances of their lives in the North?

6. What are the effects on Mikey of his privileged education? In what ways is Mikey both a personal success and a personal failure? "His parents could both see the learning was changing him, but so was the unlearning," Porter writes. What does Mikey learn and what does he unlearn, and how do the "learning" and the "unlearning" change him?

7. At the union meeting in chapter 25, the union representative quotes the union president as saying that "democracy in the labor movement, as in various segments of life, can be carried too far." What is your reaction to this statement? In what ways, if at all, can democracy—in any "segment" of American life—be carried too far? What expressions of this attitude have there been in recent American history?

8. What are the implications of the novel's final scene, in which—in the midst of a blizzard—Sam looms over his fallen son, "no more than a ghost," and in which Mikey cannot hear a word that Sam is saying? What are the implications—for Mikey's future, for the future of all young black people, and for the future of all young Americans—of the novel's final sentence: "The wind was reaching into his father's mouth, snatching his words away, sending them flying into oblivion"?

Imani All Mine

Connie Porter's eagerly anticipated, intensely affecting story of Tasha Dawson, fifteen years old and the mother of a baby girl, brings together her keen insight into childhood and her firsthand knowledge of life in the ghetto that is Tasha's home. In her own pitch-perfect voice, Tasha recounts her days of diapers and schoolwork, of jumping rope and dodging bullets. Her daughter's name, Imani—which means "faith"—is a sign of her fundamental trust and self-determination. Tasha herself, a child mothering a child, and the memorably singular characters who surround her reveal the pains of poverty and the unconquerable power of the human spirit.

1. To what extent does Connie Porter avoid presenting Tasha as a stereotypical unwed teenage mother? What makes Tasha the singular, sympathetic character that she is?

2. Porter has said, "I see *Imani All Mine* as being a kind of bridge, a way for adult women and adolescent women to have some conversations about some issues women face." What are some of those issues? Are the issues raised in this novel applicable *only* to women?

3. In what ways does Tasha become "grown" and in what ways does she remain a child? What personal, familial, social, and cultural factors influence her in both respects? To what extent is her ceasing to be a child the result of an accumulation of experiences or of a single experience? To what extent is she a grown woman by the novel's end?

4. How would you describe the relationship between Tasha and her mother, past and present? What events and what personal traits cause changes in that relationship? Why cannot Earlene show more sympathy and understanding to a daughter whose situation is so similar to what hers once was?

5. Imani reports that "Mrs. Poole say you want respect from your child, give respect to your child." How does respect or lack of respect affect the lives of all the people in Tasha's world? What kinds of respect are seen as important? What are the consequences of disrespect? What instances are there of respect and disrespect irrevocably changing the lives of the individuals involved?

6. What lessons does Tasha learn about being a daughter, being a mother, being a friend, being a woman, and becoming a responsible adult? Where and how does she learn these lessons? How does what Tasha learns compare with what you learned as a teenager? To what extent is Tasha self-taught in this regard?

7. Imani means faith, "in some African language." In what ways does Imani embody faith for Tasha? The preacher of the New Light of the Covenant church says, "You need faith. In your life. In your heart." What kinds of faith are present in the novel, and why are they important to those who profess or claim them? What is the "faith that's all mine" with which the book closes?

8. Describing the morning-after memorial to Stephan Richardson, Tasha tells us, "Seems like memorials be everywhere now.... I ain't

never seen a memorial where the person resting in peace was older than twenty-one." What do these rites tell us about the world in which Tasha lives and the world in which we live? What is the future of a community where there are so many memorials for children? What special significance does the final memorial have?

9. What is the importance of the single biblical quotation in the novel, the preacher's reading of Isaiah 40:31 in chapter 11? In what ways are the people of this book "a waiting people," as the preacher claims? In what ways are we all "a waiting people"?

FOR DISCUSSION

1. How do the chapter headings help us to understand each novel's characters, action, and principal themes? What purposes are served by the *Imani All Mine* chapter headings being drawn from children's songs and games? Do the chapter headings in *All-Bright Court* have a similar coherence?

2. What similarities and differences are there between the presentations of black families in the two novels? To what extent is family structure intact in both books, and to what extent are families in various states of disintegration? How do various forces — personal, social, economic, and cultural, for example — influence family cohesion and family disintegration?

3. Porter has said, "I think God opens doors in people's lives." What doors open for the individuals of these two novels, and what or who opens those doors? What do the characters do with those open doors?

4. What incidents of youth violence and crime occur in the two novels? How does Porter handle these incidents? How are the acts of violence in the 1960s and '70s of *All-Bright Court* similar to or different from those in Tasha's more contemporary world? What causes, consequences, and possible solutions does Porter attach to youth violence and crime?

5. At one point, Tasha loses patience and shakes Imani, "Because I was feeling like I was some kind of prisoner to her and I can't never get away." What instances are there in the two novels of characters thinking of themselves as prisoners? In this regard, how are the two novels similar or different? To what extent do you think Porter views her characters as prisoners?

6. What instances of overt and disguised racism occur in the novels? In what ways do the kinds and degree of racism change or remain the same between the time of *All-Bright Court* and the time of *Imani All Mine*? What are the effects on blacks, whites, and Puerto Ricans and on their communities? Do the characters' reactions to racism reflect historical reality? Do they suggest ways of correcting or ending racism?

7. In what ways are the personal, social, economic, and cultural issues faced by the teenagers and adults of the two books similar or different? Which of these issues may be encountered in any society at any time, and which are specific to the times and communities portrayed in the two novels?

CONNIE PORTER grew up near Buffalo, New York, the second youngest of nine brothers and sisters. After graduating from SUNY-Albany in 1981, she earned an M.F.A. from Louisiana State University and later attended the Bread Loaf Writers' Conference. She has taught English and creative writing at Milton Academy and Emerson College in Massachusetts and at Southern Illinois University at Carbondale. Her six *Addy* books have sold more than three million copies. Named a regional winner in *Granta*'s "Best Young American Novelists" contest for *All-Bright Court*, Porter lives in Virginia.

A CONVERSATION WITH CONNIE PORTER

What writers have influenced your work? Whom do you like to read?

As a young girl I loved reading stories about girls and read a number of books by Lois Lenski and Beverly Cleary. But when I became a teen, I was more interested in reading stories about and by black writers. I read Langston Hughes, Nella Larsen, Nikki Giovanni, Richard Wright, Louise Meriwether, Rosa Guy, and Maya Angelou. I very much admire all of their work and also the work of Toni Morrison, Jean Toomer, Ralph Ellison, Gabriel García Márquez, Alice Walker, Gloria Naylor, and Terry McMillan.

How did you come up with idea for *All-Bright Court*?

The novel grew out of a short story that I wrote for an assignment during my last year at LSU. At that point it was only twelve pages. I had always wanted to write more about where I grew up, and about the steel industry there. This book gave me the chance to do both.

In *Imani All Mine*, Tasha is black, and poor, and a teenager with a baby. By making her all these things, isn't she a stereotype?

Tasha is far from being a stereotype. Tasha's general description does fit that of thousands upon thousands of black girls, and this is partly the reason why I wrote this book. I grew up very poor. I'm one of nine children who were raised in a housing project, went to public schools, public universities. I feel truly blessed because of my upbringing. Never have I lost sight of the fact that as a child, because of my class and color, some people actually did stereotype me as doomed to fail. Not only me, but also every child my mother gave birth to, every child on my street, on my block, in my neighborhood. Of course, I'm talking about a time twenty-five, thirty years in the past, but I don't feel much of a shift in attitude today.

You write about black family life. How do you see the state of the black family, especially poor families?

It is easy to say that the family structure is falling apart. There are many single-parent homes. But in many cases where you find an "intact" structure, the problems of increasing violence in poor neighborhoods, the influx of drugs like crack, the increase in the dropout rate, and the lack of job opportunities make it hard for families. Parents can control only what goes on in their houses. You have true warlike conditions in some of these neighborhoods. There are some very real pressures and concerns that did not exist when I was growing up in a housing project.

How would you describe yourself as a writer?

I would describe myself as a black female writer. I surely have been black and female all my life, and now, because I am a writer, I do not want to stop describing myself in that way. I do not fear that, because there is some descriptive tag before the word "writer," I will be pigeonholed. Racism and sexism are what can pigeonhole you. They can limit, even stop you. Not describing myself as a black woman will not prevent that from happening.